NESSIAH AND DOMINICK 2: A BBW LOVE STORY

MIZ. LALA

TEXT UCP TO 22828 TO SUBSCRIBE TO OUR
MAILING LIST
If you would like to join our team, submit the first 3-4
chapters of your completed manuscript to
Submissions@UrbanChapterspublications.com

This book is dedicated to LOVE. Not that we just met, and ya penis is long, hitting every wall I have love. Not the damn your vagina sounds like I'm stirring a pot of macaroni and cheese love.

No, the real, underrated, can I take you out on a date love. The I sent these flowers just because it's Wednesday love. The I knew you were the one, love at first sight love.

This is my ode to love. To love, that is pure, that is rare. Love that never manipulates. Love that never comes when you call, but is always on time. Love that never makes you cry. The kind of love that's always done when it's spoken. Love that can be a listening ear, a shoulder to cry on. Unconventional, Unconditional LOVE!

I hope to experience you one day, if the Lord is willing!

~Miz. Lala!

1

CYBER HERMÉS

Reality Check

The low growl coming from the back of Jazmine Sullivan's throat filled the room as she sat at her vanity mirror getting dressed for her next set. Cyber had been on the run from her previous life for the past six months. After her hot and steamy affair with bad boy of the 'D', Yakhi Rodriguez, she returned home from her impromptu road trip later that night to her angry girlfriend, Layah Montross, who had broken into her house, and waited for her return.

That night they practically destroyed her little apartment, head to head in a fist fight like two bitches in the streets, instead of two overly-damaged women who fell in love with the brokenness they both possessed. Battered and bloody, Cyber had no one to turn to, so she packed her bags, hopped in her car and headed to the airport. Not having an initial plan of where she was going, she arrived at the ticket counter and brought a one-way ticket to the first plane that was leaving well after midnight, that ticket was purchased for a new life in South Carolina. Who in the hell decides to start over in South Carolina? Nobody. And that was the exact reason she picked the lonesome state. She knew that the first place her friends and family would look would've been in the more popular states like Georgia, New York City, Las Vegas, Florida or even Texas. She wanted to move somewhere where she would've been under the radar.

That was exactly what she got when she first touched down there. It was an adjustment; one she welcomed with open arms. It didn't take her long to find a decent, one-bedroom studio above an art gallery. After penny pinching for the first three weeks, she decided to hit the pavement looking for work. Just like when she was in Michigan, the idea of becoming a stripper crossed her mind. Being that there weren't many strip clubs in South Carolina, she jumped on the first one she saw. When Cyber was a little girl, she hated her looks. She was always teased and bullied in elementary school for her masculine features. As time went on and the older, she got, she learned to embrace what the good Lord had blessed her with.

Working at the Landing Strip, her exotic features were the main attraction there. Majority of all the exotic dancers were white or Latina, so she became the club's secret weapon, only after working there for a month. On average,

Cyber made anywhere between two to five thousand dollars a night, and that was before she took her clothes off. She was starting to see that South Carolina wasn't so bad after all.

IT WAS GOING on two o'clock in the morning, when Cyber arrived home from the club. She was dog tired. Her feet were swollen, her lower back felt like someone had set fire to it and don't even mention the tightness in her belly. Cyber had made some tremendous adjustments to her sets and her attire at The Landing Strip. Her new alterations always left her extra tired because of the façade that she had to keep up with, so when she walked through the door, all she wanted to do was strip naked, take a hot bath and unwind.

As she walked through her apartment, the silence and loneliness greeted her. It was nights like that one when she wished she had a sane lover. She was starting to regret ever leaving Michigan. When she left, she didn't predict how lonely she would be. All she was focused on was getting out of dodge. Every time she thought about going home, it was Yakhi she thought about running to,—not Layah.

It was only in her mind that she entertained the thought of him and her together. Out loud, she wasn't allowed to mention him nor the feelings she had for him. She shook her head as she thought about the mess she'd created. Cyber was supposed to be a lesbian. She wasn't supposed to give the male race an afterthought. But there she was, standing underneath the shower head, caressing the hood of her clitoris, wishing that the fingers bringing her so much pleasure belonged to him. She whimpered as her body burned with need. She desperately wanted his short but thick body on top of hers.

Cyber shut her eyes tighter as the heat from the hot water caused goosebumps to spread down her arms and into her nether region. His deep voice in her ear as his muscle dove deep within her played on repeat in her mind. As his hot breath graced another part of her body, her fingers became taut, massaging her swollen pearl faster than before. And just when her climax was on the brink of no return, her fingers started to ache from the way she had them bent inward. A loud squeal left her mouth as she became frustrated.

"Eek."

Her eyes opened and zoomed in on the matte black tiles on the wall in the shower. The warm water beating down on the crown of her head, had her heavy and wet, dark brown hair streaming into her eyes, as she tried to regulate her breathing. Cyber stood there for five minutes just staring at nothing on the wall until she finally got herself together. She shut the water off, grabbed her terry cloth robe and wrapped it around her thick, soaking wet body. Her thick frame tracked water from the bathroom to her bedroom.

She was so content in her daze that she didn't mind the water penetrating her dark, wooden floors. She trekked over to her vanity. Taking a seat, she picked up her cellphone. Going into her old messages, she located the number she was looking for. Dialing it without a second thought, she listened to the line as it connected and then started to ring. After the fifth ring, someone picked up the phone.

"Hello?"

Cyber said nothing as she listened to the woman breathing on the line.

"Ummm... Helllloooooo?"

Still, she said nothing.

"Baby, somebody is playing on your fucking phone again." She heard the woman say, as her voice became faint.

Cyber could hear ruffling on the other end of the line, and then the sweetest sound ever created filtered through the line into her ear canal. The sound instantly soothed her aching heart. She could listen to his voice all day, every day.

"Hello?"

Cyber started to get choked up, thinking about how stupid she was to have just up and left, cutting him and everyone in her circle back in Michigan off.

"Look, stop calling my muthafuckin' phone if you ain't

gon' say shit. You been doing this childish shit for the past six months. Let the shit go."

The call disconnected and the tears she tried to hold in broke, racing down her face. It was true. Every night for six months straight, she would pick up her phone and dial his number, just to hear his voice. In the beginning, he would answer, and they would just listen to each other breathe on the line. Then she would hang up once she got her daily dose. Then one day, out of the blue, some woman answered. That night, she almost died. In her mind, he was supposed to wait for her to get her twisted ass feelings together. She had no right to get upset that he'd moved on, but she didn't care. She was pissed that he decided to give her dick away.

Cyber sat on her bed and contemplated calling him back to, confess her feelings for him, but she wasn't in the mood to make a fool of herself. Instead, she dialed her best friend's number.

Ring. Ring. Ring.

"Hello?"

Cyber held the phone in her hand as she broke down, sobbing into the phone's receiver.

"Who the hell is this?"

"Hiyyyyyaaaahhh. I—I wa—was so stupid," she cried.

"Who the—Cyber?"

"Hiy, he's moved on. Totally forgot about my ass," she huffed, wiping the constant falling tears.

"Cyber, where the hell are you? You've been MIA for

six damn months, got my gotdamn nerves all over the damn place."

"I—I had to get away. I never meant to stress you out, though."

"Yes, the hell you did! Yo' selfish ass couldn't even pick up the damn phone to call and at least let me know you were alright?

"Hiyah, you don't understand. I had to leave. If I didn't, I probably would be in jail right now, or dead."

"What the hell are you talking about?"

"The night when Khi came to get you, we went for a long drive, and we did something we shouldn't have. Once we returned back to his place, I snuck and went home after he told me not to. When I got there, Layah was there waiting on my ass. I didn't even get in the door good, and she was wailing on my ass. I fought back, though. We were going at it, until one of my neighbors came knocking at my door, telling me that he'd called the cops."

"Again, you couldn't pick up the fucking phone and call me or Yonei?"

"I honestly wasn't thinking. By the time I realized that I hadn't phoned anyone, I was already seated on the plane, about to take off. I thought everyone would've been better off without me around."

"See, you chose to make that decision. No one said they didn't want you around. You assumed that bullshit."

Cyber had gotten quiet. She wanted to ask about Yakhi

so bad, but she didn't want her best friend to think that he was the only reason she called to begin with.

"And he's doing awful. Masking his emotions and gallivanting around the hood with this half breed, Chinese, monkey looking bitch. You need to bring your ass home and come get your nigga before you end up losing him to this hoe."

Cyber cleared her throat, glad that her best friend hadn't given up on her and was still riding for her.

"Is—Is she prettier than me?" she whispered.

"Bitch, hell nawl. I just told you the hoe looks like a hot ass mess."

Cyber chuckled at her overly-dramatic ass. It was comforting to know that his new joint didn't have nothing on her. Then again, the girl could've been pretty, but Yakhiyah made herself believe the girl was ugly because she wasn't her best friend.

"So, when are you coming home?"

"I can't do that. Ya brother not fucking with me like that, so there's no point in coming back."

"Girl, fuck him. Bring ya ass home. You had no business up and leaving no damn way. Hell, you missed that girl's damn funeral, Cy."

"I know, I know. I just couldn't see her laid up in a casket like that. Fucking bastard," she mumbled. Just thinking of her good friend, brought tears to her eyes once again. "I'll think about it. I just don't want to be around him while he's with her. And let's not even think about running into Layah," she said, palming her forehead.

"Girl, boo, Layah in a whole new relationship with some white bitch," Yakhiyah said, disgust lacing her tone.

Cyber's head started to hurt after hearing that piece of information. It seemed like everyone was living life and being happy while doing so; all but her. She was stuck in a whole new state miserable as hell, but what did she really expect? Somewhere deep down inside of her, she wished that time stood still for those in her life, like it did for her. That realization hurt her feelings.

"Well, I'm not going to hold you on the phone While I have my internal pity party. I just needed to hear your voice. And again, I'm sorry for making you worry about me."

"That's what real sisters do, Cy. You can come home at any time. Nobody is standing in your way but you!"

"I hear you. I'm about to go to bed. I had a long day at work, and I'm exhausted."

"Well, okay. I love you, Cy, And remember, you can come home anytime."

Cyber ended the call and laid her head down on the porcelain top of her vanity. When her head raised up, a sparkle caught her eye, and the stinging sensation in the back of her eye rushed to the surface of her pupil.

"How did my life get this complicated?" She pondered.

2

YAKHIYAH RODRIQUEZ

Forever Ain't Promised to No-damn-body!

Yakhiyah was sitting inside of London Chop House awaiting the arrival of a potential client for Eye for Fashion, where she worked as the editor-in-chief of the upscale magazine. She took out her rose gold compact foundation case made by Fenty beauty, and checked her appearance. Deciding not to go to the restroom to touch up her lipstick, she did so at the table.

"Sorry for my tardiness. I had a business meeting that ran over schedule," the gentleman with the deep voice said, as he stood over her.

Yakhiyah was so into fixing the small smudges of her lipstick underneath her bottom lip, that she almost didn't hear him as he hovered over her. Looking up, she damn near wiped lipstick all over her bottom teeth.

The man that stood before her was so tall and attractive, she was at a loss for words. He stood around six feet seven inches tall, with olive tanned skin that looked as if he'd stood out in the sun for hours. He had over a dozen moles and freckles battling against each other, to see who would be victorious in covering his thin cheeks. His dark, brown eyes gave off a mysterious, seductive glare, that made her thighs clench.

Her eyes trekked over his suit jacket and just knew his abdomen had to be chiseled. After the brief pause at his midsection, her eyes traveled up to his piercing, dark, brown eyes. His features were so exotic, it was hard to describe them to you. He put you in the mind of the male model Carson Aldridge.

"Is it alright if I sit down with you?"

"Yeah—yes, sure, you can sit down."

"How are you doing, mama?" he asked, removing the burnt brown suit jacket that matched his slacks.

Yakhiyah's eyes bulged at the plentiful tattoos that covered his, and neck. Never in her life did she think she would find a Caucasian man so attractive. Instantly, her mind drifted off to his penis. She wondered if it was small and raw looking. The thought of his pink penis trying to penetrate her, made her stomach turn. What woman didn't like the feeling of being stretched out, or the feeling of a man deeply embedded in the bottom lining of her vagina?

Her thoughts were interrupted by his warm, callous hand, brushing against her knuckles.

"Are you alright?" the tone of his voice sent shivers

down her spine. *How could someone who looked like him sound so thugged out?* She wondered.

"Yes, I'm fine. I just have a lot of stuff on my mind."

"You should let me handle that for you."

"Excuse me?"

He sat up straight in his chair, eyes dark and alluring. He bit the lower left corner of his lip, then leaned forward, hands clasped together.

"I said you should see someone about that."

Yakhiyah's eyebrows hiked up and then lowered, as she tried to figure out if her mind was playing tricks on her.

"Yeah, I'll think about you—I mean, I'll look into it. I'll look into your idea," she said, shaking the unwanted thoughts out of her head. "So, Mr. Green, what qualifications do you possess, and what is your background?"

"It's Luka, and I have my bachelor's in communications. I've interned for Koi McRobinson's podcast on CRKR radio. I've also worked as the lead radio program controller at WJLB." He smiled, showing off the platinum, diamond grill on the bottom row of his teeth.

Yakhiyah moved her hands underneath the table. She placed them between her legs,crossed her legs together and leaned forward with her fingers interlocked. A tactic she used to apply pressure to her harden clitoris.

"Interesting. So why do you want to work for E4F?"

"To be honest, I wanted to get underneath you."

"What?"

Luka gave her a weird look before he repeated himself.

"I said, to be honest, I wanted to train underneath you. I've heard some really dope things about you, and I've read several of your pieces from the Beauty Beyond The Spotlight section in Wayne State's magazine."

Yakhiyah was truly impressed stunned beyond words. She didn't think that her love for fashion and writing would inspire someone else. That's basically the premise to living in a peaceful world. There is nothing wrong with aspiring to walk in the footsteps of someone else to help you find your niche. But as a dominant race, we're so used to dimming the light of others out of fear that we'll no longer be 'popping', we don't try to help one another. In essence, that's the reason why there's so many black on black crimes being committed in America. There is enough room at the table for all of us to eat, but we have so many greedy people walking up to the table, trying to secure two seats with one ass.

"Well thank you very much. I'm quite flattered that I was able to inspire someone such as yourself."

"Why, because I'm white, mama?" he asked, licking his lips.

"And on that note, I'm going to the restroom. I'll return shortly."

Yakhiyah hopped up from the table, almost knocking the waiter over, who was carrying a tray of ice water and a few alcoholic beverages.

"Oh my God, I am so sorry" She said, as she tried to dry his shirt with the linen napkin from the table."

"He's all right. It's his job to get water and other fluids spilled on himself. You said you had to use the ladies' room, so go handle that, and I'll help him out," Luka said, standing to his feet.

Yakhiyah just stood there in disbelief. She didn't know if she should've been offended or turned on by his tone of voice and the way he spoke to her. She stared at him for a few seconds, and then turned on the heel of her nude, suede, Azar pumps, walking off to the restroom.

Once she made it inside, she stalked over to the mirror and eyed herself. The beige see-through blouse paired with the black, high-waisted slacks gave off a vivacious meets professional flair. Her eyes fell down to her wide hips, that prompted her to turn to the side, until her fat butt was in her view. The plumpness and its round shape were everything. Most women would kill their mother's and then sell their souls for her voluptuous figure.Her small waist, meaty-toned thighs and sought-after breast gave her the ideal body type. She leaned over the sink and turned the chrome knobs until the warm water ran a constant stream down the drain. Cupping both hands together, she flicked the water into her face, hoping it would cool her pulsing kitty down.

When her eyes darted to her reflection, she could see her flawless makeup job was ruined. Grabbing a few paper towels, she began to wipe the smudged makeup off her face. When she was satisfied with her bare face, she walked out of the restroom and returned to her seat.

"Sorry I took so long. It was a long line in there," She lied effortlessly.

"It's no problem, mama. It's your world, I'm just living in it," he said, causing her to blush.

She sat down and scooted her chair underneath the table. "Okay, so where were we, before my impromptu potty break?"

"You're so beautiful, you know that?"

A smile a mile long broke out onto her face. She had to admit snowflake had some game. "Thank you, Mr. Green."

"Luka, call me Luka, mama," he said, biting down on his lip again.

"I think that's unprofessional of me. I already agreed to meet outside of the office."

"And what's wrong with having an innocent business lunch?"

"There's nothing wrong with it. I usually like to keep things professional, so the lines don't get blurred."

"Yeah, I bet you have all the niggas chasing after you, huh?"

Now wait a minute, did he just say nigga? Hell, yeah, he did! but why am I not offended?

Why are my hormones racing like this? Yakhiyah questioned herself.

"Look mama, I'm sorry if I offended you."

"I'm not offended, but I prefer if you didn't use that word around me, or any other male or female of color."

"You're right. I apologize."

"It's quite all right. Now, did you bring a copy of your resume?"

Luka reached into his binder and produced a three-paged resume, sliding it across the table and into her hands.

As she looked over his credentials, she could feel his heated stare burning a hole through her forehead. Unable to take the awkward gawking, she raised her head and looked at him.

"Why are you staring at me like that?"

He shrugged his shoulder, and then replied, "You should let me take you out tonight."

"What? Umm, I don't think so," she said as her eyes lowered back down to the paper in front of her.

"I think you should. It would be a really good look, and you'll be giving me the opportunity to redeem myself."

"Why do you feel the need to redeem yourself?"

"Because I know my comment got under your skin, and I really want you to get to know me. I'm not a bad guy."

"I never said you were a bad guy, and I told you not to worry about your comment. Just don't let it happen again," she said with her head down, avoiding his glare.

"Okay, but you should still let me take you out on the town."

"Look Luka, as much as that sounds like a good idea to you, it's really not. I don't mix business with pleasure."

"You really should. How about this? how about I write

down where I'll be tonight, and you just so happen to pop up there and we run into each other?"

She started laughing at his preposterous idea. "No thanks."

IT WAS GETTING LATER and later, and somehow, Cyber had called and talked her into "popping up at The Bottom of The Barrel"; the bar that Luka would be at.

"Cyber, I don't want to be out here looking all thirsty and shit. And this outfit is way too revealing."

"So, you gone sit around crying over Saafiq until all the meat in your ass starts to droop?"

That was a name she hadn't mentioned in a long time; — six months to be exact. After he walked out of her house the morning after they had sex, she hadn't heard from him since. Every now and then, she would hear him in the background with Khi, or he would be at his house. On those days, she opted not to talk to her brother or drop by for a visit.

Saafiq had come along and brought sunshine to her stormy life. He made her smile in the short amount of time that they spent together. But the same nigga that came with the sunshine, also brought the rain. She rolled her eyes at the countless, sleepless nights and the crying fest she held every night. Just thinking about how she just recently stopped thinking of him on an every day basis, had her adjusting the boobie tape that held her bare breasts up underneath the light blue jean jacket with the furry trimmed collar.

Her hands ran over the matching light blue jean shorts made by Prada. Her eyes scanned her shoe game. The tall, jean high heels, compliments from Fashion Nova, really set the outfit off. She couldn't help but feel like a bust down Thotiana, but she'd be lying to herself if she didn't say she looked damn good. With her long, honey blonde tresses tossed over her shoulders, a deep part down the middle and her baby hairs smoothed down on her forehead, she was ready to do some damage.

She arrived at the bar around eleven pm. After hearing Cyber bash her for not wanting to go because of Fiq, she finally left out the house. Yakhiyah was sad that her two best friends weren't there to stand by her side, as she tried not to look so desperate. Several times from the walk to the car all the way until she made it to the bar, she tried to coach herself to turn around and go home, but she didn't. The nagging feeling in her chest was threatening her from enjoying herself, but despite that, she still found herself walking into the door of the bar and scooping the scene.

Yakhiyah walked straight to the bar and ordered three shots of Patrón, tossing each of them straight down her throat. She bobbed her head to 24\7, a track by Meek Mills featuring Ella Mai. Her eyes scanned her immediate surroundings looking for Luka.

"You lookin' for me, mama?" A bright smile covered her entire face, as she stood with her back to his chest.

The warmth of his breath had her slightly leaning back into his embrace. His long arms reached around her waist and enclosed her in a tight hug.

"I'm glad you showed up. I honestly thought you weren't going to," he said, as he brushed her hair from the right side of her head to the left side.

"I started not to come," she said, tilting her head back, so that she was close to his ear. The loud music posed a problem for the couple as they had to stand damn near on top of each other, just so they could hear the other speak.

"Well, I'm damn glad you came out. You lookin' good as fuck, queen." His warm fingertips glided up her exposed torso, stopping just underneath her breast bone.

Yakhiyah stood up straight and immediately wished she hadn't. Those three shots had started to take effect on her balance. She felt like her head was bobbing in a swimming pool filled with liquor.

"I'm going to run to the restroom."

"Either you have a urinary tract infection, or you're dead ass dodging me," he whispered in her ear.

Her elbow came back crashing into his abdomen.

"Shut your ass up!" she said, grabbing the back of his head, before she walked off.

Strutting across the dance floor, her hips wound to the beat of Tamar Braxton's *"Wanna Love Me Boy."* The juke box was slapping and Yakhiyah was glad it wasn't some ole whack ass bar playing whack ass songs. Her thoughts were interrupted when she spotted those familiar cognac colored irises staring at her.

Sitting on the hi-top section of the bar, he sat up straight. The beige, red and white plaid Burberry bomber jacket gave his already buff chest an added boost. He was sitting there looking like a yummy dose of caramel infused chocolate on steroids.

His eyes traced her figure like a young kid tracing a figure eight on a dot to dot worksheet. His intense glare had her forgetting the fact that she had to use—well, forgetting the fact that she'd told Luka that she had to use the restroom. She glided on her heel and turned around, headed back to the bar, unsure if he'd really seen her, or if she was tripping off those shots she consumed.

"Well, that was fast," he said as he noticed her walking up to the bar.

"Yeah, there was a long line for the bathroom," she muttered, trying not to look over her shoulder. "I'm suddenly not feeling too well. Do you want to get up out of here?"

"Yeah, we can go, mama, here you wanna go?"

"Anywhere—,"

"Aye, let me get three shots of Crown and three more shots of Patrón."

The tiny hairs on the back of her neck stood up, at the sound of his voice.

"Come on, let's get out of here."

"You ain't gone take ya shots, before you go, Ya-Ya?"

Her eyes rolled hard up into her head at him feeling as if he could address her.

"You ready to go?" she asked Luka, as she interlocked their fingers together.

"Aye, folk, my name Fiq. How you doing?" Saafiq said with his hand extended in Luka's direction.

She turned around with the most atrocious glare one could muster up. She couldn't believe that he was standing there all calm, cool and collected like he didn't break her heart. She sized him and the woman that was on his arm up. Instead of dignifying his response with one of her own, she pulled Luka away from the bar and headed for the entrance.

So much for a fun night out with somebody new!

3

O'SAUM LORD MATEN

A Bitter Pill To Swallow

His eyes burned a hole in the side of her head, as he too sat at a very far distance, watching the one that had gotten away, with someone else. O'Saum just knew he was the shit. His attitude and the way he carried himself was a dead giveaway to anyone he crossed paths with. He felt that since he was a big shot representative for the corporation, Global 1 INC, a multimillion-dollar pharmaceutical company, he didn't have to respect people's time and feelings.

Ever since his promotion last year, he'd been sleeping around excessively. He was already seeing the mother of his child, Amanda, prior to meeting Yakhiyah seven years ago. So in his mind, he wasn't cheating on Yakhiyah. He was cheating on Amanda, who had his three-year-old son, Diezel. He was doing a fairly good job of keeping the two separate, until Amanda had found out about Yakhiyah, and demanded that he took her to the house they shared. Her request had come at the perfect timing.Yakhiyah was due to go to New York's Fashion Week, so the plan was to bring Amanda by the house, let her see it and then take her back to the subsidized two-bedroom apartment she shared with their son.

Again, that was the plan, until Amanda wanted to go inside and see the décor. Looking at the décor turned into them rolling around naked in the bed he shared with Hiyah. He damn near shitted out a leprechaun, when he saw Yakhiyah sitting on the landing of their stairs. During their seven years together, they'd had their share of arguments, and he'd seen her get upset, but that day, she was in rare form. Never in a million years, did he think she would up and leave,let alone stab him seven times with a serrated steak knife. He thought he was going to die, and if it had not been for Amanda's scary ass calling the police, he just might've.

While O'Saum was laid up in the hospital, he was pissed off that Yakhiyah hadn't called or came by to see him. After all, it was her fault that he was in that situation. He became infuriated once his lawyer, River Daniels, told him that her lawyer, Mega Daniels, had put a PPO on him. He was pissed because it was obvious that he'd retained the wrong Daniels.

In his warped, sex crazed mind, he thought that Yakhiyah should've been apologizing to him, for stabbing him. The next time he saw her was at their court date, and she had the nerve to be upset with him. Everyone who had a negative opinion about O'Saum was just jealous that they weren't in the same position that allowed them to have access to multiple men or women at one time. O'Saum thought that he did nothing wrong, and he couldn't understand why Yakhiyah chose to end their relationship. But after six months, he wasn't over what she'd done to him. Not only that, but Amanda was acting like a bitch, choosing not to be with him either, even keeping his son away from him.

So, he sat at the bar watching the woman who ruined his life walk away unscathed. He picked up his Heineken and brought it up to his lips. His mind was racing with different thoughts, all of them focus solely on hurting her and bringing her to her knees, begging for his forgiveness.

He grabbed his jacket off the back of the chair, tossed a few crumpled up bills on the bar top and rushed out, in hopes that he could catch up with her. Just as he arrived in the parking lot, he saw them walking toward the valet parking line. Before much thought could be put into approaching her, his feet had already taken off.

Quietly he strolled a few behind them, trying to pick up on their conversation, but they were speaking too lowly. Just as they were getting ready to get in the an all black, 2019 Audi RS 3, he called out to her.

"Yakhiyah!"

Watching her plump behind from the back, he couldn't

help but grab his crotch. He waited for a few seconds before he called her name again, because he was certain that she hadn't heard him.

"Yakhiyah!" He said a little louder.

He watched as she slowly turned around. As he got closer to her and her date, he was able to see her face more clearly. His feet stopped their stride, and they just stood there looking at each other. The feeling of regret instantly washed over him. He was starting to feel stupid for ever fucking her over.

If he was being honest with himself, Yakhiyah was the only woman he'd ever dated that treated him like a king. No matter how many times he talked down to her, hit her or cheated on her, she remained loyal to him. She was the first woman who took his vision about his dreams seriously. She really loved him, and he ruined that with his lying, manipulative ways.

"Why are you speaking to me?" she said in a flat tone.

"Damn! after seven years, that's how you speak to me?" He asked, confused.

"After seven years of pain and bullshit? Yeah, that's how I speak to you," she spat.

O'Saum bit the inside of his cheek. He was mentally telling himself not to slap the piss out of her disrespectful ass.

"Why haven't you called me, hell, or came back home?"

"I thought you would've gotten the hint, but I guess I was wrong to assume. When I packed my shit and left, that was my cue to you that I was done with you," she said with her hands clasped in front of her.

"We both know that you'll never be done with me."

"Aye, blood, if it wasn't obvious, she's moved on, so I suggest you do the same."

"And who the hell are you to be addressing me?" He asked in confusion.

"First off, don't address him. You're not even supposed to be within fifty feet of my personal space. If I wanted to be an ignorant bitch, I'd call twelve and tell them that you're harassing me."

"Bitch, ain't nobody—,"

"Don't fucking disrespect me. I stabbed your ass seven times because you disrespected me. Don't make me add seven more lashes to that ass," she said, walking away.

Not liking the way, she tried to emasculate him, he grabbed her forcibly by the arm and was met with a powerful blow to his jaw, knocking him to the pavement.

"I'm not the queen. I'll shoot your ass next time. Once again, for the last time, move on blood. Your life could depend on it!" The tall, wannabe black-white gangster said, as he walked away with the woman who still had a hold on his heart.

"Walk away now, but the next time you'll be walked to your final resting place. Stupid, bitch." He said, spitting blood on the cement in front of him.

4

SIONEI

You Can't Stay Here!

Sitting in the front seat of her Lexus IS, she clutched her chest as the gaping wound in the center of her chest leaked that familiar red substance, we all needed to survive. The hot tears drained from her eyes and fell rapidly onto the black one-piece she was wearing. Outside of her shallow breathing, she could hear her ex, Izzoni, ranting in the background.

"Fuck, fuck, fuck! You made me do this shit, Yon! I told ya ass, you tried to play a nigga like shit was sweet or something."

Her mind started racing as she tried to remember how a seemingly exciting day turned into this. Love had all the traits of karma. If you played with it and didn't truly cherish the one you were with, you could end up in the same situation as Sionei. As the life started to slip out of her, she closed her eyes, while her mind started to replay how her love story turned into a tragedy.

Glass from the corner of the windshield shattered everywhere. The blow back from the glass hitting her in the face confused her. With glass and blood in her face and near her eyes, her head darted to what was left of her front window. She sat up some, straining her eyes at the grainy object fifteen feet in front of her. She leaned a little closer, and that's when she heard another gun shot. Right after that, she felt the burning sensation in her chest. She looked off to the left of her and saw Izzoni standing there zoned out.

In her mind, she was taking off her seat belt in a hurry, but her hands hadn't even made it to the red button on the buckle, before the blast from another bullet forcibly pushed her back against her seat, penetrating her flesh once more. Totally in shock with the taste of hot metallic staining her taste buds, her hand slowly moved to her mouth instead of the seat belt buckle.

Why is my mouth bleeding? She wondered. Her mind reeled on their conversation before all of this happened.

"Look, I think that it's best if we just move forward and leave the shit where it's at. I can't trust you, and I don't think I'll ever be able to again." "What the fuck are you talking about, Yonie? I made a fucking mistake and I'm trying to fix it, but you trippin' talking about you don't trust me."

"I'm not tripping, I don't trust you. You claim it was a mistake, but we were dealing with each other for six months.

That's half a damn year. And during those six months, not once did you think to come clean about your relationship status."

"You right, I should've told you, but you didn't ask either."

Shocked covered her face as she looked at him. She just couldn't believe that he had said that to her.

"Wow, so since I didn't ask, you didn't think to be a man and tell me? What kind of fuck shit is that, Iz?"

Izzoni blew out a frustrated breath as he looked down at the gravel that covered the parking lot. Lately, he had been on tip something serious. He knew how he could get if he blew his top, and he didn't want her to see him like that, nor did he have the desire to hurt her, so he took deep breaths to try and calm himself.

"Sionei Renea, I had no intention of pursuing you. You basically chased me. I wasn't—"

"WHAT? Yeah, I came at you, but I never would have continued to see you if you would've told me. Don't try to flip this shit on me, nigga. You know what? Just let my door go, I'm over this conversation."

Shaking his head, his hands slipped behind his back and into the waistband of his Tom Ford distressed jeans.

"I can't do that. My mind won't rest if I allow you to just walk away. I can't do that shit, Yon."

"You really don't have a choice. I don't want to have shit else to do with you, for real."

He shut his eyes tightly as he tried not to blow up on her, but Sionei wasn't backing down.

"Izzoni, let my damn door go. I'm not trying to sit out here arguing with you."

Izzoni's head slowly lifted. He pulled his hand from his pants, the barrel of the gun brushing against the back of his Ralph Lauren Bomber jacket.

SHUT THE FUCK UP! he screamed.

Sionei's head jerked backward in fear. Izzoni had never talked to her like that. The bass in his voice let her know that he wasn't playing with her.

"I tried to be nice about the shit, but you fucking blew that shit. You say you don't want to be with me? Well, you've only got two options, the way I see it. You either give me a chance to make shit straight between us, or you can't stay here,"

His extended arm was firmly planted an inch away from her face. Her eyes filled with fluid as she stared into his wild, dark, beady, brown eyes. The only thing running through her mind was that no matter how much time you spend with a person, you never truly get to know them. Not once did the thought of her losing her life cross her mind as she stared at the red and chrome plated Desert Eagle with a cross and bones imprinted on the rubber grip of the handle.

"I can't let you go knowing you're still on this earth, existing without me. Shit can't rock like that, my baby."

"So—so, you're going to kill me if I choose not to be with you?" she stuttered, petrified.

His shoulders rose and then fell, giving off the impression that taking her life was based off the choice she made.

"Wow. Wow, wow, wow, wow, wow," she chanted over and over.

Tears slid down her cheeks as the realization hit her. Silence covered them, each of them in their own minds, drowned out of reality by their thoughts.

"So, what's it going to be?"

Her head turned slowly as she took a real good look at him. Her eyes veered off and she looked straight through her windshield. She remembered the sound of a truck pulling into the parking lot from the north side of the entrance. It parked rather oddly in the middle of a row of parking spots. Because of the grave distance, Sionei couldn't see what the person looked like, but she could tell that the person was a woman, based on her hairstyle.

The stranger's hair was long and flowing around her shoulders. The slenderness in the person's face also corroborated her theory of the person's gender. Her eyes were trained on the object in the woman's hands when she so foolishly said, "Do it, kill me."

The next thing she knew, she heard gunfire.

Bow! Bow! Bow!

The realization that she was shot finally settled into her brain, within a few minutes of being shot. The panic was replaced with anger. It was hard to focus on the many questions that swirled through her mind. But that last question made her throat clench. *Am I going to die?*

As the blood ran from her mouth, her conscience screamed

at her. "I don't wanna die!""I just wanted someone to love me, I didn't wanna die for it.""Lord, I'm sorry, please don't let me die."

Tears eased down her eyes as her blurred vision returned to Izzoni's tensed face. She could see him looking down at the gun in his hand, and then over at her.

"Izzy, please," she whispered.

When he didn't move, she concluded the end.

"My life in exchange for your love," she mumbled, as the light switch of her life turned off.

"Yon, are you listening to me?" Izzoni asked, as he leaned over into her car.

Seeing that her face and the entire front of her shirt were saturated in her warm blood, he started to panic.

"Baby, wake up. Come on, wake up, beautiful." He said, patting her face with his fingertips.

He looked down at the gun in his hand, trying to figure out what the hell happened. His eyes then darted over to her sunken face. Stuffing the gun in his coat pocket, he placed his fingers on her neck where her carotid artery was located, but felt nothing. Not accepting the reality in front of him, he moved his fingers to her limp wrist, feeling for a pulse that wasn't there.

"BABY, I DIDN'T MEAN TO. I—I THOUGHT, I—I'M SORRY, PLEASE GET UP. YONIE. YONIE." He screamed as the tears raced down his face like a fleet of horses.

"YONIE, PLEASSSEEEE!" he pleaded as he violently shook her lifeless body.

His mind veered off as he used his huge hands to try to

stop the blood that was steady seeping from the holes in her chest. In a fit of rage, he must've blacked out, pulling the trigger three times.

The sound of cars leaving the parking lot, brought Izzy back to the present. His head turned from left to right, as he scoped the area around her car. His heart started racing, as the thought of him being seen came to mind. He looked over at her and kissed her on her midnight blue painted lips. Holding his lips on hers for five minutes, he leaned up and whispered in her ear.

"I love you so much. I don't know what happened. I thought I unloaded the clip, Yon, I swear to God. Baby, I'm sorry!"

He stood up and looked around. The location of her car was parked toward the back of the parking lot, where there wasn't that much traffic. His eyes lowered to her closed lids, as he allowed more tears to fall from his eyes. He closed her door and looked around once again, as he pulled the hood down further over his head.

Walking away from her car, he located his truck and hopped in. Without hesitation, he started his ignition and sped out of the parking lot, burning rubber, as he left the scene.

5

YAKHI

I Don't Love These Hoes

Yakhi was sitting in his most lucrative trap counting money with Synclaire and Saafiq by his side. For the past six months, they'd all been on their grind, serving kilos by the boatload to the streets. They all seemed to be going through something in the relationships they had with the women in their lives. Although each of them had thrown themselves into their work, no one was majorly affected by their problems except for Yakhi. Sure, they were all in their feelings, but Yakhi felt Cyber's betrayal in his soul. Not a man of many emotions, it blew his mind that he'd opened up to her and allowed her into his world, only for her to go running back to her pussy ass girlfriend.

"Aye, nigga, we need to get into some shit tonight!" Synclaire said as he ran two stacks totaling $34,000 through the money counter.

"I'm wit' the shits." Saafiq said, thinking about the last time he seen Yakhiyah.

It was a struggle for him every day. Every day he worked in close quarters with her brother, and he always had to swallow the urge to ask how she was doing. He had told himself to leave her be, until he grew the fuck up.

"A nigga dead ass doesn't feel like partying tonight," Yakhi said, as he sparked up another Backwood.

"Nigga don't never wanna kick the shits with his day ones, ever since he got wit Aoki's funny looking ass," Synclaire stated, as a chuckle slid through his deep, purple lips.

"Nigga, fuck you. Everybody don't wanna be up in the fucking club every weekend sack chasing with these hoes."

"But yet you wifed up a sack chasing hoe," Synclaire said, shaking his head.

Part of his statement held some kind of validity to it. Aoki wasn't known for tricking throughout the hood, but she definitely had multiple bodies underneath her Hermès belt. Aoki was a smart bitch, she had her own job and made her own money, but she liked to be spoiled by spending other niggas' money, and she never turned down a gift. She had really laid on the charm super thick when she ran into Yakhi. He was so secretly broken over Cyber's sudden disappearance, he couldn't even see that she was using him for all his money.

"Man, chill the fuck out on my lady, G."

"Okay. But let me ask you this. When was the last time

y'all went out and she picked up the check?" Synclaire inquired.

"When was the last time y'all went to the mall and she offered to buy you some shit from outta that bitch?" Saafiq chimed in.

Saafiq had noticed Aoki's scheming ways as well, but he wasn't trying to pick a fight with Khi over the bitches he spent time with. Sure, he looked at Yakhi as one of his younger brother's, but in life, we all had to bump our heads before we learned the valuable lesson that was presented at the end of each chapter in our lives.

Yakhi, not wanting to go back and forth with them about shit he already knew, decided to keep his mouth shut. He had long ago, peeped her selfish "gimme this, gimme that" personality, but he liked her company and she was the only one who knew the real definition of "fake it 'til you make it". Or so he told himself. The real reason he kept her around was because he knew what it felt like to be alone. The first month that Cyber was gone was the hardest. He stayed to himself, only going out to make his money and then he was right back in the house. He wasn't even visiting his sister, and he did that two, sometimes three times, a week. Yakhiyah wasn't having that shit though, she would pop up on his ass in a New York minute.

As the months flew by, he slowly got over the feeling of being alone and got back out on the scene. When Aoki came along, he fought tooth and nail to stay away from her. That experience hardened his perception of women and relationships. All a bitch could get from him was a nut, and maybe a meal from Burger King. Ultimately, it was her persistence that swayed him.

Yakhi didn't mind spending money on her, it was the fact that she was so greedy and selfish that bothered him. Everything his brothers said about her was true. But because he didn't want to revert to the depressed Khi, he let her stick around.

Hearing the ringing from his cellphone ended his mental trip. He stared at the unknown number and let it continue to ring, until it eventually stopped. That relief was short lived as the caller called back once again.

"Nigga, why the fuck you sittin' there on stuck, watchin' ya hitter ring and shit?" Fiq asked.

Yakhi didn't say a word. He had an inkling of who the caller could've been, but he wasn't for sure. Every time his phone rang, he became paranoid. The calls had started six months ago. He would answer and the caller wouldn't say anything, just breathed into the receiver. He used to sit on the call for over fifteen minutes just listening, waiting for the person who he thought was Cyber to say something,—anything. But as always, as soon as the timer on his screen hit fifteen minutes, like clock-work, the call would disconnect.

He had gotten tired of the shit. With the caller not saying anything for six whole months, he started to doubt himself. He knew that Cyber was probably fucked up behind the shit she did, but he thought that if it was her, she would've apologized by now.— Sadly, he got nothing of the sort.

"I don't know who the fuck that is. They just call and sit on the phone then hang up." He said, as he ran more money through the counter.

"You think it's wifey?"

Yakhi chuckled at Synclaire's attempt to be a smart ass. He as well as Saafiq noticed the change in his attitude once Cyber left. To his surprise, they were very supportive of his unresponsiveness and the disappearing acts. Their loyalty to him was what made him love them as hard as he did. He would die for his niggas, and they would shoot it out until it was lights out for him too.

"Naw, I don't think it is," he said somberly.

Just that fast, he was upset. Pissed off that after all this time, just the mere mention of her had his mood switching up like he'd missed one of his doses of his bi-polar medication. He shook his head at the thought that he was still in love with her scurvy ass. Why else would her sudden departure after their brief moment of meeting each other, bother him so much?

At first, he had a point to prove to himself, then the point was flipped on her. He just wanted to show her that he could push her to the limits of her willingly having sex with him. She was so sure that she wouldn't like dick and that his dick couldn't or wouldn't make her submit to any man, but they were in for a rude awakening as his dick barely penetrated her.

That night, Yakhi's little lesson plan was interrupted by Yakhiyah, but the little bit of performance he'd given her left a lasting impression on the them. There were times where he would stand under the shower head masturbating to the images of her underneath him. Hell, 85% of the time he was sexing Aoki, Cyber was the inspiration behind him finishing.

His mind would travel back to that very night, and he would create the perfect ending. His hand ran down the front of his face, as he scolded himself for letting his mind go there once again. There weren't many times he allowed the thought of her to cross his mind, but when it did, he'd feel fucked up about it, and become pissed off all over again.

It was well after five in the afternoon, as Yakhi and his guys showed up to some rooftop party that was held in Midtown. The party had been advertised on all the most popular radio stations in the D, Hot 107.5, Channel 955, Kiss 105.9 and WJLB. The party was a black-tie affair, so everyone in attendance was wearing black, well, almost everyone. Aoki showed up at his apartment on the westside, wearing a white pants suit. He shook his head as he opened the door because black folks just didn't wanna follow simple fucking rules.

When they arrived at the party, he immediately ditched her and went searching for his crew. At the bar stood Saafiq and his flavor of the week, Kelania, as well as, Synclaire and his ole lady, Amaraa. He had called his sister earlier and asked her if she wanted to come, but she declined. He was starting to get pissed off with his twin. He felt like some shit was up with her because she was never available anymore. She was always too busy to hang out with him, and with him being in the streets more and cuddled up with Aoki afterward, they hardly ever got to see each other. That shit was unacceptable!

Yakhi stood around just shooting the shit with his clique, enjoying the rare moment where they could kick back and not have to worry about if a shipment arrived on time, if it had made it safely to the warehouse and if it was distributed correctly. That was a sporadic occurrence, so he was going to enjoy the festivities.

Yakhi was standing off to the side of the railing overlooking the beautiful landscaping down below the terrace, when he saw something shimmering in color entering the rooftop from his peripheral. Turning his head in the direction of the object moving around, he saw someone standing near the entrance dressed in a short, silver and gold sequined dress, with nude pumps on her feet.

Since the person's back was to his front, he couldn't see who the it was, he couldn't help but to be drawn to the fat ass that was sitting on her back. He couldn't figure out why he couldn't take his eyes off the back of the person standing 50-yards away from him.

"Nigga, where ya mind at?" Fiq asked him, as he nudged him in the side.

Yakhi shook his head and turned his head back around, so that he could rejoin the conversation his friends were engaged in. They all conversed for a few more minutes, until he saw movement again from his peripheral. As he went to turn around, he was hit in the face with the sweetest smell, and then the voice he was so familiar with flowed through his ear canal.

"Oooh, this place is nice. Hi, big head." He heard, and then felt a bump to his hip.

Yakhi turned and came face to face with his twin sister. Yakhiyah was dressed sexily in a black fitted tuxedo jacket, fishnet stockings and hot pink, suede, closed-toed pumps on her small feet. At first glance, it appeared that she had no bottoms on underneath the jacket. But when she turned to the side, you could see the black, diamond encrusted bottoms that resembled cheer spank panties. He reached over and pulled her into his warm embrace. As he kissed the side of her temple, his eyes drifted off to the last person he expected to see.

Cyber stood there clothed in the short, silvery-gold dress he'd been staring at since she appeared out of nowhere. She stood there sipping on what appeared to be a ginger ale, looking unbothered. His eyes ravaged her frame. She was still thick as a bowl of cold grits, but he could tell that something was definitely different about her since he'd last saw her. Even her hair had switched up. It appeared longer, as she wore it in a short, feathered bob haircut. Their eyes locked and held an intense glare. Everyone in their small circle noticed the intensity in the shift in the mood. That was made apparent when Aoki stepped up and introduced herself to Cyber.

"Hey, my name is Aoki, I'm Yakhi's girlfriend," she said with her hand outstretched toward Cyber.

Cyber smiled at Aoki and then reached her hand out to shake hers back. Yakhi blew out a tensed breath, because he just knew that Cyber was going to say some crazy shit. He was glad she was acting like a classy woman out in the public eye.

"Nice to meet you as well. I'm Cyber, Yakhi's wife." Cyber finished, flashing the French cut, nine carat, halo, diamond encrusted wedding ring that was weighing her ring finger down.

"Checkmate!" Yakhiyah whispered into her brother's ear.

6

SAAFIQ

No Love Lost

Saafiq stood in the cut as the bullshit started to pop off. He had seen Yakhiyah when she first stepped through the door. His eyes were so fixated on her barely clothed body, that he missed the fact that she had Cyber with her. The urge to approach her was intensifying. It had been six long months without seeing her face or so much as a hi over the telephone.

He knew that she had been dodging him. Several times he had met up with Yakhi on the days he was going to visit his sister, but because Yakhiyah knew he was with her brother, she wouldn't answer the door. He was just sitting back biding his time, trying to give her some space. But the night he'd run into her at the bar with her little company, he knew he couldn't sit back and wait any longer.

Saafiq had been in his head for the past three weeks,

thinking about when it would be the right time to not only tell Yakhi that he was falling in love with his sister, but to also ask him if it was cool if he dated her. Normally he wouldn't have given a fuck about asking a nigga for permission to take a girl out and fuck her brains in, but Yakhi was his brother.

When he touched down from Atlanta to Detroit, he thought he was just coming to learn how Khi was moving in the streets, but what was supposed to be a one-time business deal, turned into a tight bond of brotherhood. So out of respect for him being his little brother from another muva, he was going to sit down and rap with him.

Finally making his mind up to go speak to her, he was stopped in his tracks by the corny ass white dude she was at the bar with. He was leaning with his elbow on the corner of the makeshift bar top the club had up on the roof. His eyes locked on her and the guy that had just walked in the door, as he sipped the lean from his cup. Saafiq watched enviously as the two flirted back and forth with each other like they were the only two people in the room. He wanted so badly to go snatch her up by her arm, and whisk her away from the party, just so that she would hear him out, but he didn't want to cause a scene. He wasn't too fond of catching a DV case, all because he wasn't man enough to give her the love, she so badly deserved.

∾

THIRTY MINUTES HAD PASSED and Saafiq was ready to go. The Promethazine a.k.a "dirty sprite" coupled with the zannie bar he'd popped had him feeling heavenly. His night would've been perfect if the woman of his dreams was on his arm and not the next (white) nigga's. He watched as Yakhiyah went to intervene in her brother's bullshit.

Deciding to make his move, he pushed himself forward, and walked toward the couple, grabbing Yakhiyah by her elbow, then escorting her toward the stairs that lead back into the club.

As they walked up the stairs and outside to the sidewalk, they remained silent. Turning to face him, she finally spoke.

"Was that necessary?"

He pushed the buffs up on the bridge of his nose, as he tried to focus his dilated pupils on her.

"You really out here violating something serious, sweetheart."

Yakhiyah crossed her arms over her chest, bored by his words. "I don't know what you're talking about, but if you wanted to have a conversation with me, you could've politely and respectfully, introduced yourself and asked my boyfriend if you—,"

Saafiq's neck craned backward, as her words finally started to register in his mind.

"Politely introduce myself to your boyfriend?" he asked for clarification.

"Yes, politely and respectfully asked my boyfriend if you could speak to me."

"Sweetheart, I ain't about to ask another muthafucka if I can have a minute of my bitch's time. You trippin' folk!" he chuckled, offended that she let some dumb shit like that come out of her mouth.

"Your bitch?"

"Yes, my bitch," he said slowly, as he tried to close the distance between them.

Holding her hand out, Yakhiyah stopped him before he could come any closer to her. The way her hormones had been on one for the past six months, she knew that if she allowed him to step into her personal space, she would've been face down ass up over the arm of that man's console in his whip. She didn't want to do that. She had vowed to hold on to her silent journey of celibacy.

Saafiq looked down at her and his eyebrows furrowed. He didn't like that she wouldn't allow him to get close to her. In his mind, that was a signal that she wasn't fucking with him like that anymore. And that wasn't an idea that he could get used to.

"I'm nobody's bitch, let's be real fucking crystal clear about that shit! Don't you ever fucking disrespect me like that again, you fucking asshole." She said, punching him in the chest.

She turned to walk away, because she wasn't one of those women that put her hand on a man. She didn't do domestic violence of no kind. She felt it was necessary for her to walk away, because Saa was taking her out of her character. She didn't get too far away, because his long, muscular arm had captured her tiny waist and moved her into his space. Her eyes involuntarily closed, as she fought to hold on to her self-control. It was hard though. The warmness that covered her from head to toe had her getting comfortable and forgetting about her secret vow to herself.

"Saa, let me go." She whispered as his head nuzzled the soft skin in the crook of her neck.

"I'm sorry, Ya-Ya. A nigga dead ass missed the fuck outta you, gurl," he said, placing small butterfly kisses up her neck, until he reached her helix.

Again, she tried to step out of his embrace, but he stopped her. His jaws tightened as he tried to check his emotions. He had to tell himself that he had to relax. He was cause of the state of their relationship. He kept repeating to himself that he couldn't be mad because she knew her worth. But damn it if her resistance to be around him didn't fuck with his ego.

Saafiq wasn't one of those guys who couldn't admit when he was wrong. He didn't try to fuck with a woman's feelings. Often the women he had a mutual agreement with regarding sex, were on the same playing field as him. No connection, just straight sex.

"Saafiq, let me go." she said a little bit louder.

"Let you go so that you can go back to your boyfriend?" he asked, pushing her out of his embrace.

"What I do with my time and who I do it with, is my business," she said, glaring up at him.

His frown deepened as the thought of her going off and being happy with sweet vanilla inside the bar, burned him deep in the center of his chest.

"Nawl, that's not how shit rocks with me, shawty. You can't get a nigga back like that."

Yakhiyah just rolled her eyes and walked back into the establishment, leaving Saafiq standing on the sidewalk rubbing his beard, with his crushed feelings at his feet. If she thought that he was just going to give up and allow her to be happy with the next nigga, she was in for a rude awakening.

7

IZZONI

Living Inside A Nightmare

Izzoni barely made it into the driveway of his property, as the tears continued to cover his face. He threw the gear shift into park, as he turned the bottle of Hennessey up to his mouth. His eyes lingered on the brand-new property he'd just brought for him and Sionei. The thought of her had his mind was reeling as he thought about how he'd killed the love of his life. Just as he was about to take another drink, the ringtone for his text messages sounded.

Unknown: *Now that it's over between you and her, we can get back on the right track. Now, Izzy, I know you were upset the last time we spoke, but I want you to really think about all of this. Your answer will determine your future.*

Unknown: *Ask yourself this question; do you want to live peacefully, or do you want to be on the run looking over your shoulders for the rest of your life?*

In the last message from the unknown caller, there were five pictures enclosed. The first picture was a zoomed in image of Izzoni holding a gun toward a car. The second picture was a far away picture of the first image. The third picture was an up-close shot of Sionei's dead body in the front seat of her car. Pictures four and five, were of Izzoni leaving the scene and a close-up picture of his license plate number.

The phone fell to the floor in his car, as he hurriedly pulled his gun from his coat pocket. Snatching the glove compartment door open, he looked down at all the bullets under the clip. He grabbed the clip and looked inside of it. he confirmed what he'd already knew. Before he got out to wait for Sionei, he had removed all the bullets from the clip and the chamber. After Shreece had threatened him, he started carrying the firearm for protection. He only brought the gun with him to scare Sionei. Knowing how head strong she was, he thought he would use it to scare her into being with him,

He'd tried everything he could think of to get her to talk to him, but sadly, nothing worked. Not even this idiocy plan. From the conversation, he didn't have to ask who it was that was texting him. He knew it was Shreece that had fired the fatal bullets into Sionei's car. In his state of confusion, he thought maybe it was his gun that had killed her. That maybe he hadn't taken all the bullets out. Now he knew the truth. Picking his phone up, he sent out a text for confirmation.

Izzoni: Who the fuck is this?

Unknown: *Who do you think it is?*

Izzoni: Shreece?

Unknown: *Bingo! You wanna know what your prize is? ME!*

Bingo is right!

Taking another swig of the dark cognac, he exited out of his messages and went to his keypad. Opening it, he paused and inhaled a harsh breath. Saying fuck, it, he dialed three numbers he never thought he'd use in his life. Especially not in a crazy ass situation like this. Pressing call, Izzy placed the phone to his ear. He waited the three seconds it took for the phone call to be answered.

"Hello, Grosse Pointe Farms police department. What is your emergency?"

"I—I need you to listen very clearly. This call won't take long, but I need you to really listen to me without interrupting me. Can you do that?"

"Sir, are—,"

"Can you do that?"

"Ye—yes sir, but sir, you sound like you're intoxicated."

"I just said I need you to listen. Now what is your name?"

"My name is Laurie, sir."

"Laurie—Laurie, that's a pretty name, Laurie," he said, taking another drink from the fifth he tightly clutched in his hand.

"Tha—thank you, sir. What seems—,"

"My name is Izzoni Savage. I play point guard for the Dallas Mavericks in the NBA. Is—is this call being recorded?"

"Yes, sir, all of our calls are recorded. Why don't you tell me what the problem is? I don't want to assume that this is some drunken, prank call. If it is, you could be cited and placed under arrest for—,"

"This isn't a prank call. This—this is my confession."

"A confession? What is it that you feel the need to confess to?"

"I was engaged to a woman by the name of Shreece Montgomery. We dated for a little over two years, before I started seeing a woman by the name of Sionei Miller. I was madly in love with Sionei. I had just broken things off with Shreece six months ago. She had found out about Sionei from our phone bill." Izzoni paused to take another swig of the alcohol. Wiping the remnants that slid down the corner of his mouth on the back of his hands, he continued with his tale of his twisted love affair. "Sionei had actually found out about Shreece a month before the phone bill incident. I was at a game in Chicago, when Shreece proposed and Sionei had came to the game. Probably because I had cut her off four months into the affair."

"I only cut her off because Shreece started acting like my woman again. She was doing all the things I wanted her to do; cooking, cleaning and making love to me on the regular. You know, that kind of stuff.""Anyways, Yonie cut me off. She wouldn't answer my calls or let me see her. A nigga was dead ass going crazy behind her little short ass." He chuckled. "Today—today was the first time I had seen her in six months. She was looking so damn good. Her skin was glowing, and she looked genuinely happy, without me."

Laurie, the police dispatcher, sat quietly on the line as he rambled on about the two women he was seeing at the same time. At one point during his story, she had to mute her line as tears clouded her vision. She had long ago, stopped transcribing the conversation and just let the recorder pick everything up. The pain in his words proved that he loved the young lady, Sionei. The feeling in her chest told her that something bad had happened.

"Anyways, I popped up at this warehouse that I knew she would be at for a photoshoot. She posted that information on her Snap chat account. So, I went up there and waited for her to get done. When she came walking out, she kind of brushed my presence off."

Click. Click. Click.

"What is that noise?" Marylynn whispered over her shoulder.

Nudging her away from her, she tried to focus on his words. She wasn't concerned with what sounded like he was tapping on the screen.

"I really tried not to let her disinterest in me being there get to me, because I knew I was the cause behind her cutting me off. But that didn't mean that the shit didn't affect me. I can admit I was drinking before I went to see her. I'd been drinking ever since she ended our relationship.""I was irrational. I threatened her and, told her if she didn't take me back, I was going to kill her."

The gasp that left Laurie's mouth had Izzy's stomach turning. Just hearing how bad everything sounded, had him breaking down all over again.

"I—I wasn't really going to kill her. I had taken the bullets out of the gun before I approached her car. But as the argument started to escalate, there were— all I heard were gun shots. Her windshield shattered, and—and there—there was blood all over her. I kept looking at the gun thinking that it misfired, or that—that – there was another bullet in the chamber that I'd missed."

Izzy exhaled a jagged breath. His head was spinning as he started reliving the events that had just taken place.

"I—I kissed her lips and then closed the door to her car after I apologized. I left the scene of the crime and drove home. I just received a text message from Shreece basically confessing to killing my soul mate."

And that was it! Izzoni broke down and cried from the depths of his soul. A gut-wrenching scream left his lips as the realization that he'd never see her again, crossed his mind.

"Sir—sir, I need for you to calm down, okay?"

"How can—can I calm—calm dow—down, when the love of mm—my—my life was just murdered in front of me—because of me?"

"Sir, I understand that, I really do, but I need you to get a hold of your emotions and—,"

"I—I can't! I don't deserve to live. I've robbed the world of something so precious, and I have to pay the price for that," he said as he loaded all the bullets, he'd taken out of the gun earlier, back into the clip.

"Now sir, listen. I understand that—,"

"You understand? Lady, you don't understand shit! The aching pain in my chest, you couldn't possibly understand that. I want to thank you, Laurie, for letting me vent. I really appreciate you, mama."

"Izzoni, listen to me. Please just listen to me. Although this tragic thing has happened, that doesn't make you a bad person. You have no control over how others will conduct themselves—,"

"Byyyeeeee, Laurieee." He slurred his words.

He took the safety latch off the gun and placed it inside of his mouth.

"Izzoni?"

One...

"Hello?"

Two...

"Izzoni Savage? Marylynn, please call back up. Izzoni?" Laurie said in a shaken tone.

Three...

"Izzoni, this is Captain Gregory Lawton. Son, can you hear us?" The captain asked, as he seized the receiver from Laurie's hands.

Four...

With the phone in his lap, Izzy mentally counted, as he got ready to pull the trigger. In the distance, he could hear the sirens. With his eyes closed tightly, he could see her vibrant smile, the way her hair flowed in the wind. The look of pleasure she would give him when he was buried deeply inside of her. The saddened look on her face the night Shreece proposed to him, and how her face dropped when she saw him standing next to her car. And finally, the way her eyes rolled up inside of her head, as she took her last breath.

"I loved her, I swear I did."

Five....

"Izzoni, son, can you hear me?"

Bow!

The loud, piercing sound could be heard over the phone in the call center. Everyone within proximity of Laurie's cubicle, had tears in their eyes, as they stood nearby, listening to the call since it first came in.

When the fire trucks and the six police cars arrived at the end of Izzoni and Sionei's driveway, the sight of red blood covered the back windshield of his truck. The two officers that cautiously approached the driver's side door both leaned over and spewed huge chunks of vomit next to the tires of the vehicle. Izzoni sat slumped over, with a hole the size of a Cucumber melon in the back of his head. There was brain matter and pieces of his skull all over the windows and the head rest.

Officer Reagan opened the driver-side door and retrieved the phone from his lap. Grabbing a Kleenex from his pocket, he touched the home button on Izzoni's Iphone screen. On the screen was a blank text chat with no phone number. Inside of the text box was a picture of what Shreece looked like, her cellphone number, the address to her new house, her mother and father's address, the color, year, make and model of her car. Officer Reagan showed the lit-up screen to Detective Marsh. The words *I'm sorry* were captioned below the information. He grabbed his notebook from his pocket and jotted down the information.

"Call Jerry West in the tech department and have him put a trace on this woman's cellphone. If she uses it, her location will pop up on one of the cell towers. Also, get Amy and Geraldine to run a background check on a Shreece Montgomery."

Everyone stood stagnant where they were. They were used to suicides, but never one of this magnitude. There wasn't a dry eye nowhere on the scene. Love was a drug of choice and if you weren't careful, death could be the only cure.

8

SHREECE

I'll Do Anything for His Heart

Shreece had just ended her phone call from her mother as she stood in line at Charlotte Russe inside of Fairlane mall. She knew she should've gotten out of the area for a few days, but she just couldn't turn down a quick mall run. Being one of the lead Registered Nurses for Detroit's Children's hospital inside of the Neonatal unit, she wasn't afforded the luxury of having too many days off where she could come browse the stores and find really cute pieces.

So, what was supposed to have been a twenty-minute shopping trip, turned into an hour long shopping trip. Charlotte Russe was going out of business, and she wanted to stock up on all the cute, affordable things before they were all gone. She soon realized that was a big mistake, as she watched women of all different colors and sizes swarm all 1,089 sq. feet of the store.

As she stood in line, she noticed two men walking into the store. The way they were looking around, caused her to be on alert. She started questioning if her impromptu trip could've waited. Her nerves started to soar, as the possibility of the men being police officers crossed her mind. The issue wasn't because there were two men in the store. No. Men came into stores like Charlotte Russe all the time for themselves or their women. It was their demeanor that had her shook.

She blew out a deep breath, and she coached herself. Izzoni wouldn't call the cops on her.

"Just calm down, Shreece. He would be incriminating himself if he did call them," she whispered to herself.

She turned her head as they neared her, When she turned her head toward the back of the store, the television that was mounted above the dressing rooms caught her attention.

"Just in, we've just gotten word that basketball star, Izzoni Savage from the Dallas Mavericks, just committed suicide a half hour ago. We were told that he called the Grosse Pointe Farms Police Department and confessed to the killing of his girlfriend Sionei Miller—,"

"Meagan, I hate to cut you off, but that last detail was incorrect. Mr. Savage confessed to witnessing the death of his mistress, Sionei Miller."

"My sincerest apologies. Well, since you have more

information than I do, Dan, why don't you finish reporting the story?"

Meagan Strokel, news anchor for WXYZ, snatched her microphone from the front of her blouse and stormed off the set, with the camera catching every glimpse of her dramatic exit. The screen then cut and panned back over to Dan Harper, senior anchor at WXYZ.

"Well, the GPF's officers on the scene revealed that Savage sat in inside of his 2019 Range Rover in front of this house, that sources says he purchased for he and Ms. Miller, and held a forty-five minute conversation with dispatcher, Laurie Shields, as he confessed to bringing an unloaded gun with him to the Fashion District downtown to scare the young lady into taking him back. During an argument with Ms. Miller, gun shots rang out, striking the victim and killing her almost immediately."

Shreece felt like someone had sucker punched her in the gut. The back of her neck got hot, as anger filled her system rapidly. Tears played peek-a-boo with her eyelids, as what the news had reported ran rampant through her mind like an intense game of Foosball. The details shuffling back and forth, had her wanting to break down. She couldn't believe what they were saying. She told herself that she wasn't going to believe it. Pressing the button on her screen, she opened her call log and pressed Izzoni's contact.

"You have reached the automatic voicemail system for (313)—,"

Shreece hung the phone up, and dialed the number again, as the warm salty tears dripped down her face and onto the phone screen.

"You have reached the—,"

"You have reached th—,"

"You have reached the automated voicemail system of—,"

"You have—,"

Calling his phone back to back, she was met with the same result. Her mind ran wild and her stomach started to turn just thinking about the fact that he was dead. Her eyes bugged out of their sockets as they alleged that he had killed himself because she killed his little girlfriend. Those facts slapped her hard in the face.

"I know this motherfucker didn't. Naw, he didn't," she whispered to herself, as she tried his phone once again.

Her eyes scanned her surroundings looking for the two suspicious men that had entered the store a few minutes earlier. When she couldn't find them, she decided that she needed to get out of there. Shreece stepped out of the line and sat her merchandise down on the shelves near the check out line. As she walked to the door, she continued to call his cellphone repeatedly. Making it just in front of the threshold, someone grabbed the back of her arm.

Turning on the heel of her Giuseppe Zanotti wedged heels, she looked into the eyes of one of the men that she thought could've been the police.

"Is there a reason that you have your hands on me?"

"As a matter fact there is. My name is Detective LongJón with the Dearborn police, and I would, like to ask you a couple of questions down at the precinct."

"Answer questions about what, sir?"

Her heart rate had reached dangerous levels as the room around her began to spin. *What the hell did they want to speak with me about?* She wondered. Then the thought occurred to her that while Izzoni was laying down his burden by the riverside, he'd told on her as well. Why else would he have killed himself? He didn't want to go to prison, and he damn sure didn't want her getting a hold of his snitching ass.

"We just want to ask you a couple of questions about your fiancé, Izzoni Savage." The shorter detective of the two spoke up.

"Well, I don't know what's there to talk about. Izzoni and I are currently separated and, have been for a few months now."

"Well, we would still like to ask you a few questions down at the station."

"You can ask me whatever you need to right here."

"We need to go down to the station, ma'am."

"Am I under arrest?"

"No, ma'am, we simply want to—,"

"Well than I respectfully decline to come down to the station. I watch enough of Law and Order SVU and Criminal Intent to know how your questions will go," she said, walking out of Charlotte Russe.

As soon as Shreece made it out of the store, she started speed walking to the parking lot. Once she located her car, she wasted no time jumping inside and burning rubber as she pulled out of her parking spot. She was in such a hurry, she was oblivious to the speedometer as it reached fifty-five miles-per-hour, and that was before she could even put her seat belt on.

Shreece made a right hand turn onto Hubbard drive. The light had just turned red, when, in a haste, she sped through the light and ended up t-boning a red, 2016 Dodge Journey SUV, that housed a woman and her two kids. The impact from the crashed had thrown the toddler who wasn't securely strapped into her car seat through the windshield and out into oncoming traffic. Several cars that were traveling through the intersection, as the accident happened tried to stop their vehicles, but it was no use. All three cars ended up hitting her small body.

Shreece watched in horror as one by one, all three cars hit the little girl, each time sending her twenty-five-pound body flying from one hood of a car to another, until she finally found rest in the middle of the intersection of Evergreen road. Screaming to the top of her lungs and banging on the steering wheel, Shreece started to have a mental break down. As if that wasn't enough commotion for the day, the sound of a police siren behind her had her resting her head on the steering wheel. Shreece looked over at the gun that was lying under the floor mat in the passenger side. She closed her eyes as she silently wept.

"Why me, Lord? All I wanted was for him to love me," she whispered.

The curdling screams of the young woman, had Shreece covering her ears as she rocked back and forth, trying to soothe herself.

"She killed my baby!"

"I didn't mean to. I swear I didn't mean to!" Shreece screamed.

"Alana. Alana, please wake up. Alanaaaaaaaa!"

"I'm sorry."

"Go arrest that bitch, she killed my babyyyyy!"

"Oh my God, I said I was sorry!"

The woman screamed to the top of her lungs.

A loud tap to her window, had her abandoning her method of comfort, and looking over at the window. Just outside of her car door was Detective LongJón, the cop from the mall. She rolled down the window, as he lowered his hat from his head.

"Shreece Montgomery, you are under arrest for the murders of Alana Jordan and Sionei Miller."

Shreece hung her head as she talked to God.

"Lord, please forgive me for my sins."

9

ARLYSE

You know who talks the most shit? The bitches who shit not together.

"Throw that ass back and stop playing with the dick, Lyse," he said as he slapped her hard on her smooth, round buttocks.

She whimpered as he pounded aimlessly away at her sweaty flesh. She winced as he called her every foul name in the book. Her mind drifted away, thinking back on how her life had gotten so messy. There was a time where she would sit back and indulge in the 'tea' of everyone else's lives, never thinking that one day her own piping hot tea would be the talk of her friends and family.

"Man, what the fuck you doing? Yo' ass begged a nigga to come over and yo' ass zoning the fuck out, like you doing me a favor, by letting me hit."

"I'm not zoning out, baby. C'mon, fuck me harder,

daddy," she moaned, as she began to thrust her hips from underneath him.

It was as if every second of the day for the past six months, she'd been asking herself that same question. It was hard loving a man that didn't love you back. That was her reality.

Six months ago, she thought she was living in a fairytale. As her helicopter landed on the roof of the venue her and her fiancé had chosen to wed at. The whole day was magical, from being waited on hand and foot, to the lavish never-ending gifts. Those moments were fit for the queen of India. If it was even remotely possible, her head and her attitude had grown seven feet tall that day. She was so busy with her nose up in the air, that she wasn't privy to the tale tell signs that were looming around her. If she was, she probably could've saved herself the heart ache and humiliation.

"Fuck this shit, I'm out." He said, pulling the used condom off his deflated penis, chucking it on her gold and black Versace duvet blanket.

With a disgusted look on her face, she sat up, clutching the other end of the blanket up over her exposed breast.

"Why do you have to use such vulgar language?" She said with her nose turned up.

"Man, what-the-fuck-ever. You wastin' my gotdamn time with this bullshit, I could've been at the office working or at—,"

"Home, waiting by the phone, hoping that she'll call you?" She asked, sitting up on her knees.

"Mind ya fucking business." He growled, as he pointed in her direction.

Her sad eyes watched as he got dressed in haste. He was moving so quickly, like the thought of sharing another breath with her was going to kill him. The flexing of his muscles in his biceps subdued her, while her mind returned to the day her fairytale ended.

The moment she took one look at him, she knew something was off. He was distant,—distracted. He didn't look like himself. Arlyse stood there at the altar looking at the shell of what used to be Dominick Washington. All she could remember thinking as the pastor continued his speech was that he was going to back out on their deal.

"What the fuck is going on in your mind, right now?" He screamed, jilting her from her thoughts.

"You don't have to yell at me."

"Yeah the fuck I do. Yo' ass over there acting retarded than a muthafucka."

"Watch the way you speak to me," she said with an attitude.

She was tired of his smart-ass mouth. Sure, he'd been a smart ass since she met him, but these last few months had been the worst for her. He acted as if he hated the sight of her. But she was so desperate for his attention and more importantly, his money. Ever since Dominick had showed his ass at their wedding ceremony, her daddy cut her off, telling her to get a job since she couldn't keep her man.

Jackson Dubois, at one point, was the richest nigga in Detroit. He had some of the best product flooding the streets of the D, not to mention his bars that were used as a front for the underworld of illegal gambling. He had just about every powerful figure in the city in his pockets. They weren't aware of his side hustle. To them, and any other green person, the Tippy bar, was just that, a bar. But Jackson was just like every other black man dirtying up the streets with cocaine, crack, heroin and pills, he was greedy. He let his greed drain his bank account and that was the reason he made the deal with Destine. He was tired of his daughter leeching off of him. He was hoping that she had that grade A pussy like her mama did, so that she could steal money from Dominick to give to her family.

"So, you're leaving?" She asked the question she already knew the answer to.

"Yeah, I got shit to do."

"Shit to do or someone to do?"

"Doesn't matter. That's your problem, you always worrying about shit that doesn't concern you."

"And since when did worrying about you stop being my concern?"

"Arlyse, please run that bullshit on somebody who doesn't know ya ass."

"What the hell is that supposed to mean?"

"It means that I'm not stupid."

"Again, what is that supposed to mean?"

"Let's not go there. I'll hit you up when I get back on this side of town."

Arlyse stood up in all her naked glory and ran after him. "No, let's go there! what the fuck does that mean?"

He continued to the front door without paying her a second thought.

"Dominick, I know you hear me talking to you."

He turned around so fast that he scared her, and she jumped back into the wall.

"It means that your ass was never a part of this scheme because you genuinely cared about me. I know all about your father's money problems and, him thinking that I was going to be your Bill Gates in shining armor."

He walked off, but just as he had gotten shy of the front door, he turned around and looked at her. His mouth opened, as he shot daggers at her.

"Oh, and don't think I don't know about you fucking Destine behind my back. You really should stay the fuck out of people's houses, before ya ass end up buried in the backyard, with the other homewrecking whores."

Arlyse stood there with her mouth wide open. It was never her intention to get caught up fucking around with his father, but Dominick and her father had both cut her off, and she had a reputation to uphold. Her need to maintain her cushioned lifestyle wouldn't allow her to feel bad about her infidelities. Yes, infidelities, as in more than one. She was currently sleeping with Tyson, the manager at his bar Liquid Courage. Hey, a girl had to get to the bag by any means necessary. Now all she had to figure out was how to remove the pest by the name of Nessiah and she would have an unlimited supply of those dead presidents she loved so much.

10

DOMINICK

Might Have Some Fuck Nigga Tendencies

The sound of a car horn blaring behind his car gained his attention. Parked in front of H.O.P.E's building, Dominick blocked the entrance to the parking lot. His mind had veered off and found interest in Nessiah, but that wasn't nothing new. He'd been thinking about her for the past six months.

Ring. Ring Ring.

His eyes dropped down to the phone in his lap. Upon seeing Destine's name on his screen, his face bawled into a deep frown. Out of respect for him being his father, Dominick kept his distance. Not having the best relationship over the years, Dominick tried to extend an olive branch, by popping up at his parents' house out in Southfield to surprise his father with lunch, but he ended up being the one to get the surprise.

Upon walking into the house, he found it a mess; clothes and take-out containers on the floor and dinette table. His mind hadn't even drawn the conclusion that something was wrong, until he got to the top of the stairs. He was all too familiar with the moans that were being shouted from the other side of his parent's bedroom. He was so familiar with the moans that begged for mercy, the thought of his penis getting hard crossed his mind. It was like he knew what was going on. He knew it wasn't his supposed fiancée and his mother in the room, because she was on a retreat with some of her snobby ass friends. So, that left Destine. As sick as the thought was, he just had to see the act for himself.

Dominick slowly opened the door and instantly saw red. Hanging half-way off the mattress was his fiancée with her legs wide open, and his father's head buried deep between her legs. Quietly he closed the door behind him and left them to finish their indiscretion.

Dominick wasn't even upset, that the two was messing around. He was upset that his father was playing his mother. Natalie heard him loud and clear the evening of his wedding, and she had been trying hard to get their relationship on the right track. So, to keep from breaking his mama's heart, he kept his mouth shut, until Lyse tried to play him.

Tap. Tap. Tap

Dominick looked over at the young woman standing

outside of his window. Rolling the window down, he looked down at the woman.

"Wussup, shorty?"

"Would you mind moving your car from in front of the entrance?"

"Yeah, sorry about that."

"No problem. Cheer up, you're way too fine to be looking so sad." She winked and switched away to her Volvo.

Dominick looked out his side mirror at the woman's fat ass. He shook his head as he watched the wool fabric in her skirt stretching across the two watermelons that resembled her fat buttocks. He shook his head and then let his foot off the brake, allowing the car to move forward slowly. He whipped his car into one of the handicap parking spots and then turned the car off.

His eyes traveled to the woman's car, as she honked the horn when she drove by. His eyes left her vehicle and then glanced over at the building in the distance. His eyes traced each letter, as he baited time trying to get his thoughts together. His eye brows furrowed as he tried to think about how he ended up there. If he was being completely honest, he couldn't lie and say that he hadn't thought about taking the trip there. He just didn't want to play himself. He'd already done that the evening of his wedding. The way she looked at him right after he placed the wedding gown on her, was enough to make him say fuck love. Him just standing there watching her, he didn't recognize her.

The provocative, vivacious woman that stood in front of him at his wedding was a very different woman than he met three months before. She was confident and, had this positive vibe going on. The irrational side of himself refused to believe that it had anything to do with the nigga that popped up with her at HIS wedding. But then there was the rational side, that could call a spade a spade. He knew her change in attitude and the way she embraced her appearance had everything to do with dude.

He gritted his teeth as he tried not to get upset. He felt like Nessiah had played him by bringing a date to his wedding when she knew where they stood. Dominick didn't want to be rational when it came to their situation. Shit, nothing in life was fair nor easy, so yes, he did expect her to ride with him until he figured shit out. He didn't give a fuck about who thought he was in the wrong to expect her to remain loyal to him while he was married. There was no room for discussion or negotiation. What he said was law and he expected her to abide by that law. When she didn't and started curving him, he damn near gave himself a brain aneurism, with all the stress and pressure he applied to his mental health.

He shook the rejection off, opened his car door and stood up, stretching his body. He closed the door and walked toward the entrance of the building. Walking in, he headed up to the sixth floor. Walking off the elevator, he walked right up to Aoki, the receptionist on that floor.

"Excuse me, he said, startling her from picking the Spinach from her teeth.

Aoki flicked the long, green string into the atmosphere. Dominick's face scrunched up at her nasty behavior.

"Hi handsome!" She said, showing every tooth in her mouth.

"Hey, is Nessiah in?"

The smile that appeared a few seconds before was wiped from her lips. Her face frowned up at him coming there looking for her boss. Aoki had been trying to bag Dominick for the past nine months, but all her attempts to get him to notice her were in vain. He simply ignored her flirtatious behavior.

"Nessiah left a few hours ago."

"Who did she leave with?"

"Why, her fiancé of course," she said, cheesing really hard.

Dominick's face began to turn a bright shade of red, as he thought about her trying to be messy. He took a step back, turned on his heels and headed for the elevator. Stopping mid-stride, he called out to her over his broad shoulder.

"You still got that green shit wedged in between your front teeth. And next time, take ya nasty ass to the restroom and use some paper towels to wipe the shit on. Nasty bitch!" He barked.

Hours had passed and Dominick was still parked outside of H.O.P.E waiting on Nessiah to return from her lunch break. His eyes glanced down at his dashboard, where the time read 2:15 p.m. Her break had been over for an hour and she had yet to return. He was starting to think that she wasn't coming back to her office. Just as that thought came to him, his phone rang, distracting him from his thoughts of her.

Ring. Ring. Ring.

Watching Destine's name scroll across his screen had him blowing out an exaggerated breath. He had been blowing his phone up for the last three or four weeks. His betrayal to his mother was enough for him to cut him off completely. He watched as the ringing stopped and then started back up.

"Man, why the fuck you blowing my jack up like you my bitch or sum shit?"

"Boy, who the hell you think you talking to, little nigga?"

"Man, what the fuck you want?"

"Little muthafucka don't get shit twisted. Just because I've retired from the game, don't mean my muthafuckin' ways have retired! I'll come fuck ya little ass up. Show some fucking respect!" Destine barked into the receiver.

Not the least bit fazed by his father raising his voice, he

returned his eyes toward the front of the building, waiting on Nessiah to return.

"Give me sumthin' to respect and I will!"

"Fuck you just say my nigga?"

"I said give me sumthin'—,"

"Aye, real shit, Dom, I don't know who the fuck stuck they dick in ya ass this morning, but you need to dial that shit the fuck back real fucking fast and come correct. Nigga, I'm still ya fucking father."

"And? Nigga, ya ass ain't no fucking father. You just the nigga that shot me outta ya wrinkled ass nut sac. What type of father would be on the dumb shit you been on, bruh?"

"Fuck is you talmbout?"

"Nigga, I'm talking about the fact that ya ass still out here fucking around on my mama, nigga. Then to add insult to injury, ya disloyal ass fucking on my bitch at that!" Dominick barked as he watched Nessiah walking hand and hand up the sidewalk with the nigga that was at the wedding with her.

The line was quiet, as Destine tried to figure out how Dominick knew about him and Arlyse. He thought that they were being careful when they met up. It was never his intention to hook up with her, but the shit just happened.

One day he showed up at Dominick's house looking for him, to discuss when they were redoing the wedding, because Jackson had been on his ass about keeping his end of the bargain. Arlyse answered the door in nothing but a white t-shirt and tube socks. She explained that Dominick had left but would return shortly if he wanted to wait for him. Waiting for him ended up with his dick shoved so far down her throat that his dick was playing with the Fruit Loops she had for breakfast. And that was all she wrote. Whenever one or both could get away, they met up in a hotel and had hot steamy sex.

Destine had only invited her over to the house because he started to feel guilty about what he was doing behind his son's back. But like all the other times, they ended up naked and sweaty underneath each other. Shortly after the high had left his shaft, he was back in serious mode, telling her that they couldn't see one another again.

"Son, I—I, let me explain. It wasn't supposed to happen like that. I wasn't trying to—,"

"Nigga, save it! I don't want to hear your sad ass excuses. You fucked up for the last time. You got the most loyalist bitch in the D, yet you—,"

"Boy, what the hell is wrong with you? You gon' sit here and disrespect ya mother while you on the phone with me?"

"Bitch nigga please, I know damn well ya ass ain't telling me to respect her, when you haven't respected her for the past 22 years? Fuck outta here, D."

"What I do is my business. Now granted I did fuck up, but that's for me to deal with, not you."

"I'm telling my mama how foul you are. Got her out here catching bodies left and right because ya selfish ass can't be a fucking man and keep ya dick in ya pants. I think it's in your best interest to go home, pack up all ya shit and move the fuck around."

"Dominick, I know I did some fucked up shit, but I need her. I can't let her leave me. I swear I'm sorry, son."

Dominick sat there trying not to be fazed by the sound of his father's voice alternating from strong to sad and broken. Listening to his father cry was fucking with him. No matter how he felt about his mother in the beginning, he always wanted to see her happy. Just thinking about how he was going to break the news of his father's latest infidelity to her was choking him up. She had been dealing with Destine's cheating ways for way too long. She deserved better.

"Have your shit out in the next 48 hours."

"Man, Dominick, come on, son. Well, can—can I at least tell her goodbye?"

"Out in 48 hours D, or I'm coming to put ya shit on the curb like the court marshalls." He hung up the phone and put his gear shift into drive.

He drove like a bat out of hell trying to catch up to the nigga who thought he was going to take his woman away from him. He told Nessiah that they were forever, and he meant that. Even if it meant getting his hands dirty again. Something he vowed to never do, ever since he killed the dumb ass niggas that killed his grandmother.

11

YAKHIYAH

Bittersweet

Walking back into the club, Yakhiyah tried to get her emotions in check. She was pissed off because he thought that after all the time that had past, he could still demand that she give him a chance. If that wasn't bad enough, catching him out on a date with someone else only burned her even more. Yakhiyah couldn't stop thinking about him sliding in and out of various women.

Her mind questioned if he made the same fuck faces as, he did when he was buried deep inside her? Or if he praised their dick sucking skills like he did hers? Were their pussies tighter and wetter than hers? Could they take the dick better than her, without running? So many question and not enough answers were making her skin crawl. She couldn't stomach the thought of him being with another woman, so when Luka approached her and wrapped his arm around her waist, she welcomed the distraction.

"What you over here thinking about?" He asked, as he moved his muscular arm around her neck.

Over the course of a couple weeks, Luka had gotten quite comfortable invading her space. She couldn't lie and say that she didn't like all the attention he was showing her, but she knew to slow her roll and keep her guard up. That was how she'd gotten suckered into Saafiq's web, well after Mega warned her.

"I just have a lot of things on my mind," she mumbled, while her eyes followed Saa as he walked back into the club.

Standing a great distance from the front entrance, Yakhiyah could see the displeased expression that had covered his face. She rolled her eyes up in her head and turned to face Luka. She wasn't going to let Saafiq's words stop her from having fun. When she tried to put on her big girl panties and give him a shot, he missed the net, hitting the backboard.

"How about we get out of here and you can tell me everything that's on your mind?"

Nodding her head, she interlocked her fingers around his, when he reached for her hand and led her toward the door. Yakhiyah was just stepping over the threshold, when she felt someone pulling her backward by her arm. Looking over her shoulder, she could see the intense expression on Saafiq's face. Turning her body adjacent to the outer door, she gave him the perfect opportunity to wrap his arms around her neck, as he lowered his lips down to hers.

A full minute had passed, before she got the urge to push him off her. She wasn't shocked by his brash boldness, but her delayed reaction wasn't a good look. As soon as their lips broke apart, her head swiveled in Luka's direction. He stood up tall, not looking the least bit fazed. Never putting himself in the same situation, Luka didn't get upset. If he was a fuck up like Saa, he would've done the same,—maybe even worse. Yakhiyah was an exceptional woman. She was very intelligent, sweet and compassionate. She deserved to have a gang of niggas after her.

"You better not go home and fuck that nigga," he whispered in her ear.

She watched as he walked off into the crowd of people. She stood there until she couldn't see him any longer.

"Ready to go?" His deep voice brought her back to the present. She turned and walked out the door, fingers still locked with his. As they made it to the parking lot, she asked the question that kept nagging at her mind.

"Why don't you seem bothered by what he just did?"

He started his 2017 midnight, hemi Dodge Challenger. Pulling out into the crazy downtown traffic, he drove for a while before he finally spoke up.

"I'm not one to get all riled up over such juvenile

things. And before you say something, I meant his actions. Why would I be pissed when you gon' be mine anyway?"

The butterflies in her belly started swarming as she told herself to relax. She closed her eyes and asked God for a stress-free chance at love. He may not come when you call him, but he's always on time!

12

YAKHI

Our Little Secret

Yakhi sat slouched back in his seat as his eyes followed her every move. He was so pissed off that he couldn't take his eyes off her. There was something so different about her, and it wasn't just her confident personality. Something was off and it was pissing him off that he couldn't pinpoint what it was.

"So, are you going to just sit here and watch her all night?"

"What do you expect me to do?"

"How about we talk about what the hell she just said? Is it true?"

Yakhi bit down on his teeth as he tried to remember everything that happened that night. The fact that the situation happened six months ago, and they were both drunk didn't help the situation. If he didn't remember nothing else from that night, he remembered after they dropped Yakhiyah off, they drove around aimlessly, while Cyber ranted about beating Layah's ass on sight.

They drove around for hours just burning gas, and she complained about not feeling loved or wanted. Yakhi wasn't in his right mind when he took the mini detour and headed toward the Detroit Metro airport. His little impromptu trip carried them high up into the sky and dropped them off in the sandy desert in Las Vegas, Nevada. Yakhi and Cyber hailed a cab to the nearest 24-hour wedding chapel, and they were married thirty minutes after their flight landed. They walked the strip together and talked about their upbringing. By the time the sun was rising, they were dead tired, sleeping at the back of the plane, headed back to Detroit.

When they touched back down in the city, they barely made it through the door, before their clothes were thrown all over the place. That night, they consummated their union, until the sun started tilting over the horizon. Yakhi, totally sober by that point, told Cyber not to leave his house, as he headed to the grocery store to make his new-found wife breakfast in bed. When he returned twenty minutes later, she was gone, and so was their marriage certificate. Yakhi was so pissed off that he went looking all over the city for her. It was so bad that he'd put a bounty on her head for fucking with his heart.

"Yeah, it's true, but we're separated," he said, taking a

swig of the D'Usse in the clear glass that occupied his large hand.

"So, what are we?" Aoki whined in his ear.

"We're just friends getting to know each other," he said, eyes never leaving Cyber's thicken frame.

"You said that we were working toward a relationship, Khi."

"You have to be friends first, before you can become something, more, right?" He asked, eyes finally leaving his wife's sight.

"I guess, but why do I feel like you're going to kick me to the curb now that she's back in the picture?"

"Naw, we good," he said. The nerves around his eye started twitching as he watched Cyber standing some fifty feet away from him, smiling all up in a nigga's face.

His eyes dropped to the ground as he mentally tried to talk himself out of going across the room to fuck her up for playing with him. *Don't let her slut ass get to you. Nigga, we not about to stunt her ass.*

he chose to walk the fuck away, so it's her loss.

"Baby, did you hear me?"

"Babbbbbeeeee!"

His head lifted up and looked over at Aoki.

"My bad, what you say, bae?"

She sat back in her chair pouting because he wasn't listening to her. Aoki was playing her role as the caring and clingy runner up to a tee. She had no real interest in being in a committed relationship with Yakhi or anyone else. The only thing that was on her mind was the almighty dollar.

"Look, I got a lot of shit on my mind I don't have time to be trying to pacify your feelings. If you wanna have a conversation, talk. And if not, then don't!"

Aoki rolled her eyes as she watched Cyber walk in their direction. Her eyes were fixated on the woman's extended waist as she approached them. She'd always wondered what the opposite sex saw in bigger women. She knew if she was a man, she would be terrified to make love to a bigger woman, out of fear that they'd fall on top of her, crushing her into dust. She couldn't help but to roll her eyes as she watched the disrespectful nigga sitting next to her, as he watched in awe while she strutted through the crowded party, headed in their direction.

"Can I speak with you for a minute?" Cyber asked, boldly stepping in between his parted legs.

Yakhi sat further back against the chair he'd been occupying since she exposed the nature of their relationship. His eyes were on everyone and thing besides her. He wasn't trying to cause a scene at these people's establishment.

"You don't hear me talking to you?" She asked, as she reached over and mushed him in the center of his forehead.

"Bruh, don't put ya hands on me," he spoke calmly.

"Well stop ignoring me then."

"Chill out, Cyber," he warned.

"What's gon' happen if I don't?" She taunted him.

"Watch out, ma." He pushed her out of his personal space.

"You really showing out like that in front of your company?"

"Man, move the fuck around with that dramatic bullshit."

"I'm not leaving until I talk to you," she stated with her arms folded across her plentiful chest.

His eyes wandered the room, as the onlookers tried to be inconspicuous about being all up in their business.

"Cyber, stop causing a fucking scene before I get upset. You walked the fuck away, not me, so I don't owe you shit, ma," he gritted.

"You're right, I did, and it looks as if I had good reason to. Look where the fuck you at and what the fuck you're doing!"

He fanned her off, not playing into her excuse as to why she left him high and dry.

"Stop ignoring me before I slap ya ass."

"Girl, you sounding so dehydrated and looking pitiful as fuck. Damn,do he need to spell it out for you? H-E-D-O-N'T-W-A-N-T-Y-O-U-A-N-Y-M-O-R-E," Aoki said, using her fingers as if she was speaking in sign language.

Yakhi looked up as he watched Cyber close her eyes and inhale loudly. He sat up in the chair, getting ready to tell Aoki to get up so they could go. Unfortunately, Cyber halted those plans, as she sent Aoki flying out of her chair, landing on her back with her freshly shaven pussy put on blast for the world to see. Yakhi dropped his head into his hands. He couldn't really be mad at Cyber for hitting the girl and causing a scene. No one told Aoki to get in the middle of their business.

"Yakhiiiiiiii. Yakhi, are you really going to sit there and do nothing?"

He looked over his shoulder at her.

"I wish the fuck you would let the thought enter your mind to go help that hoe up. Yo' ass gon' be laying right next to her smart mouthed ass. Who's looking pitiful now, bitch?" Cyber's raspy voice came out in a growl.

"Yakhi?"

"Man, what, Oki? What the fuck you want me to say? Nobody told you to get involved. I'm a grown ass man, I can handle her ass," he said, standing to his feet. He walked over and helped Aoki up. And as sure as she was when she made the threat, Cyber bum-rushed him.

Even in a dress, Cyber was sitting on top of Yakhi's chest, punching and slapping him in the face. Not going out like some hoe, he sat up and flipped her over on her back as he straddled her waist.

"The fuck is wrong with you, girl?"

"Fuck you, Khi! I told you not to help that hoe up. You thought I was playing with your dumb ass?" She said, popping him in the eye.

He had the strongest urge to slap breath from her ass, but their mental telepathy must've finally started back working because not even a few seconds later, Yakhiyah came snatching her brother up off her friend.

"Nigga, get ya heavy ass up off my sister, fuck wrong wit' chu?" She cursed, as she put him in a full Nelson. Once she had him off her friend, Yakhiyah disappeared into the crowd.

"You know what? Fuck you, Yakhi! I came here stupidly and blinded by the stupid as happily ever after dreams I've been having since I left. I apologize for up and leaving you without an explanation. It's clear that you've moved on, and I'm not going to stand in your way. I really just came back to give you something,"

Pulling the glossy folded up piece of paper from out of her bra, she extended her hand toward him, dropping it at his feet. Yakhi picked up the small square piece of paper and looked at her as she walked away. He unfolded the square paper and instantly fell back against the back of the chair.

It was a sonogram, with the words "Congratulations Daddy!" in capital letters.

13

CYBER

The Side Effects Of You

Now that her secret was out, she felt like she could breathe easier. Cyber had been keeping her pregnancy a secret because for one, she couldn't believe it herself. And two, she wasn't sure what she was going to do about the situation. Being a mother had never crossed her mind. She had seen lesbians all the time paying women to be their surrogate, but never did she think about being a mother. Hell, as jealous as Layah was, she would probably do something to harm the baby because Cyber was giving it all her attention. She shook her head at that realization and thanked God that she didn't have to deal with her possessive behavior anymore. On the other hand, Yakhi was way worse.

She held her breath all the way until she made it out of the club. Standing on the sidewalk, she pulled out her phone and requested an Uber ride since she no longer had a car in Detroit. Cyber had just sent a text to Yakhiyah, telling her not to give her brother the name of the hotel she was staying in, when she felt a hard, firm presence in the middle of her back. Turning around, she was sad to see that it was Layah behind her instead of Yakhi.

No matter how much she tried to front, she was falling madly in love with her husband as every day rolled by. It was just something about his short, rugged ass that had her sweet, lesbian pussy juicing up at the thought of him. She hated that he had the power and determination to make her body give in to him, when it hadn't done that for no other man in her past. He would refer to it as fate, and she was starting to believe him.

"Is there a reason why you're touching me?" She asked, creating space between the two of them.

"Damn, baby, it's like that?"

Rolling her eyes, she walked down a little further from the club. She had no desire to socialize or to be seen with Layah. She was for certain that, the chapter of Layah and her was closed.

"Damn, you really feeling yourself now, huh?" Layah asked, as she neared her.

Cyber ignored her and continued looking at her Face-book page. She was silently hoping and praying that her ride would hurry up and come so she wouldn't have to deal with her. Fear consumed her as she thought about her finding out that she was pregnant.

"So, you really shitting on a nigga now, huh?"

Frustrated, she let out a rushed breath and turned her attention toward her.

"Layah, what is it that you want?"

"You!"

"Aht, aht, too little too late," she said, rolling her eyes up in her head.

"What we had will never end, you know that. We got too much history to part ways like that, ma," she said as she stood directly in front of Cyber.

"Layah, like I said, I'm straight on ever being in a relationship with you again. Besides, you've moved on, and so have I."

"Man, Chelsea just my friend. She was holding shit down because yo' ass up and ran off. She knows the real definition of a rider," Layah gritted.

"Okay, and I'm happy for you. Glad she was able to pick up the pieces."

"She knows her spot only temporary though. She knows what the fuck it is."

"But that's the part I don't get. If she was there for you like you said she was, why be so quick to cut her off chasing after something that's unattainable?"

"What the fuck is unattainable?"

"Her heart," the deep voice said, coming up from behind Layah.

Layah turned around to see Yakhi standing there

dressed down in an all-white Polo fit. He stood there leisurely puffing on a blunt.

"Who the fuck are you, nigga?"

Spit flew from his mouth, landing near Layah's fresh pair of air Jordan's. In the hood, that was a sign of disrespect. That was a man's way of telling another man that he didn't fuck with you. So, it was no surprise to see Layah pulling her 40 caliber, semi-automatic Beretta off her waist and aiming it at Yakhi.

"Nigga, I oughta blast ya maggot infested looking ass into the street, fuck nigga," she said, finger inching toward the trigger.

Yakhi stood there unfazed as he finished what was left of the grape Swisher he was smoking on. He hit the roach one last time and threw it down on the pavement.

"Layah, get that fucking gun out of his face!" Cyber barked with so much animosity in her tone.

Layah's head turned in her direction. She wasn't used to hearing Cyber talk to her with so much bass in her voice.

"Stay outta this shit, Cy," Yakhi said, never taking his eyes off Layah.

"No! Don't tell me what to do," she sassed.

"You heard what the fuck I said. Matter of fact, here," he said, pulling the keys out of his pocket as he reached his hand out to give them to her.

"Cyber, don't get yo' ass in that nigga whip," Layah gritted.

"You shut the fuck up! You don't tell me what to do either!" She said, rolling her neck and eyes instantaneously.

"Yo', you heard what the fuck I said," Layah threatened.

"Bitch, don't fucking address my wife!" He barked, walking toward Layah.

"Nigga, ya wife? Get the fuck outta here. That's my bitch, and I'll talk to her anyway I fucking want to."

"Not while she's wearing my ring and carrying my seed in her fucking stomach!"

"Really, Khi?" Cyber asked annoyingly.

Layah's bulging eyes zoomed in on the fullness in Cyber's midsection. For her to have just turned six months, she wore her pregnancy well. If you didn't know her and saw her out and about in the streets, you wouldn't have known she was expecting a child in the next three months. One would've just assumed that her belly was big because she was considered a BBW.

For some reason, her heart contracted in her chest as he outed their secret. She had no desire to be with Layah anymore, but at the same time, she didn't want her to know that she'd slept with Yakhi. Layah walked around trying to play the boss role, when in actuality, she was insecure as hell. Every relationship she'd ever had, her lover always cheated on her and made her feel inadequate. And, that's why she did and said some of the awful things she did to Cyber.

Cyber was the only real person in her corner. When

she was hungry, it was Cyber who cooked her meals, When she was tired from work, it was Cyber who gave her hour-long massages. When life had its way of bringing her down, Cyber was there to pick her up. So it wasn't that she was ashamed of letting her know she'd slept with Yakhi, she just didn't want to be looked at as another person who felt she wasn't worth loving.

"Bitch, I know you didn't—I know you didn't give my pussy away!" She screamed, lunging at Cyber.

Yakhi chuckled, as he snatched Layah up. Out of the couple times he'd run into Layah, that was the first time he'd heard her sound feminine. Guess love really was the ruler of all emotions.

"See, I'm trying to be nice, but I'ma forget ya ass is a build-a-nigga and crack ya shit wide open to the white meat if you try that shit again," he said, yanking her up by her white, v-neck t-shirt.

"Yakhi, let her go and come on!" Cyber shouted at him.

Yakhi turned and looked at Cyber with the coldest stare she'd ever seen. Cyber was starting to regret coming back to the city. Back in South Carolina, she didn't have to worry about the drama. She didn't have to be bothered with immature individuals if she didn't desire to. She obviously still cared about Layah. She was in a relationship with the girl for as long as she could remember, so it wasn't so easy to turn those feelings off. But that was something Yakhi wasn't willing to compromise on, especially not with her carrying his first born.

"Yakhi, let's—,"

"Don't say shit, just go get the fuck in the truck," he said in a low growl.

Not wanting to piss him off further, she stood there for a few seconds and then walked away. She climbed in the driver side of his Infinity Q80 truck and watched as Yakhi slapped fire from Layah's mouth, sending her falling to the ground. She shook her head as she thought that he was doing way too damn much, but what she didn't realize was that a real man would stick up for his woman. It didn't matter if it was a man or woman, if someone got flippant with him over his woman, he was going to defend her honor, right, wrong or indifferent. She watched as he started toward his truck and she couldn't help but admire the way his bow legs turned inward as he walked. She could appreciate his swagger. It was unique, and she wouldn't even bat an eyelash in the direction of any nigga that thought he could emulate her nigga in any form or fashion.

Her ogling came to a halt as he damn near ripped the passenger side door off the hinges. All she could do was shake her head. He damn near jumped in the seat, he was so pissed off. His hard stare focused on her face, and she shrank back into her seat a little bit.

"Why are you looking at me like that?"

"Don't say shit to me, just pull the fuck off."

"Okay, first off, I get that you're mad, but don't take that tone with me."

"Man, what-the-fuck-ever. Ya ass already in hot fucking water wit' me, so just pull the fuck off."

"In hot water for what, nigga?" She yelled.

"Bitch, don't fucking play like you ain't just up and leave for half the fucking year, then you pop the fuck back up flashing ya wedding ring, causing a fucking scene and, tossing ultrasounds around. Now you out here defending ya fucking ex and shit, like I won't split y'all fucking wig clean down the middle of ya fucking skull!" He screamed at her, with spit flying out of his mouth.

Cyber wasn't going to say nothing at first, but then he went and called her out of her name. She'd already went through the physical and verbal abuse before, and she wasn't doing that shit again.

"Bitch? I got ya bitch, nigga! And let's get some shit straight, I left to deal with everything that happened between us. If you can't understand that, oh-fucking-well. And I know you ain't insinuating that this baby doesn't belong to you?"

"Did you hear me say that dumb ass shit? Naw, you didn't. And ya ass ain't stupid enough to give my mutha-fuckin' pussy to the next nigga," he said, leaning over the arm rest.

He was so close to her face, his nose was pressed into her cheek. Given the awkward placement of his face, it was blocking her peripheral view through the passenger side window. He was so dangerously close, that his positioning presented the perfect opportunity for Layah to get herself together, as she started in the direction of his truck. She let her 40 Cal sing.

Boom! Boom! Boom! The first two shots penetrated the passenger side door. The third shot struck the window, shattering it immediately. Cyber was in shock as the first couple bullets pierced the truck. Her shock didn't last long as her mind finally registered what was going on. Being that she was in the driver's seat, she had a duty to protect her unborn child and her husband, who was obviously the intended target.

She threw the gear shift into drive as she peeled out of the parking spot. The fourth and fifth shot that was fired hit Yakhi in the upper shoulder blade and his ribcage as she sped out of the parking lot.

Boom! Boom!

Layah ran along-side the truck as it was fleeing, and she was able to shoot two more times. One striking the back windshield and the final bullet, grazing Cyber in her forearm.

Boom! Boom!

THREE HOURS HAD PASSED, and no word had come from the doctor on Yakhi's condition. Cyber, Yakhiyah, Saafiq, Synclaire, Nessiah, Aoki, Samuel and Racquel were all strewn around the waiting room, waiting on some kind of word. It was unexceptionally quiet and all Cyber could do was rock herself and her baby back and forth. She blamed herself. If she would've just walked away when he first told her to, maybe none of this would've happened. Or maybe if she would've drove off as soon as he got inside the truck, he wouldn't be laid up in some hospital bed fighting for his life. All different scenarios ran through her mind, as she tried to think back on the last few minutes of her life when everything was decent in her world.

The shooting was all over the news, and Cyber felt sick about it. With the kind of lifestyle that Yakhi, Synclaire and Saafiq were in, they couldn't afford to have the cops sniffing around them. When twelve came to ask her some questions, mainly who shot her husband, she told them she didn't know. She was really stuck and didn't know how or who to be loyal to. Here her husband was, sitting on the other side of the hospital dying from the bullets her ex-girlfriend had shot him with, and she was still protecting Layah. She felt like the whole situation was her fault. Had she stayed in SC, Yakhi wouldn't have gotten shot, and Layah wouldn't have felt betrayed by her selfish antics.

Cyber looked up as she wiped her tears to see Racquel, Yakhi and Yakhiyah's mother, mean mugging her. His mother and everyone else was standing around when the police were questioning her about what happened. The only one who didn't seem to have an attitude was her best friend, Yakhiyah and Nessiah, the girl who had contacted her about working for Dominick's photo shoot. Over the course of three to four weeks, they had really built a bond.

Cyber eventually had to tell Nessiah that she couldn't model in the shoot because she was expecting and Nessiah insisted that she come to the venue to be photographed.

Her eyes crossed the room and she wondered why the hell the dumb bitch even decided to show up. As his wife and Power of Attorney, she basically called all the shots regarding if he lived or died. And that meant that when he did wake up, Aoki wouldn't be seeing him. She tried to keep her anger at a minimum, but it was hard, especially seeing the bitch her man was keeping company with bawling her fake ass eyes out. Anyone with two decent eyes could see that the bitch wasn't really crying, and if she was, it was because she was afraid that if Yakhi died, so did her funded lifestyle. She gritted her teeth out of anger, when their eyes locked. The smirk that graced her face told her that her little stunt was fake as hell.

"Why are you here?" She spoke loudly.

Yakhiyah and Nessiah looked up at each other and then crossed over to the other side of the room.

"Excuse me?"

"You heard me. I said why are you here?"

"I'm here because Yakhi is my man, why else?" She snapped, rolling her neck at Cyber and then looking down at her nail beds.

"I think you need to leave," Cyber stated in a calm tone.

Unbothered by her suggestion, Aoki continued to sit there and fiddle with the rhinestones on her fingernails.

"I'm really trying to be nice. I asked you to leave, and to

leave right now."

"Look, I don't know what your problem is sister wife, but I'm not going—,"

Cyber stood up and walked toward the entrance of the emergency room. Nessiah felt as if something was off, so she turned to say something to Yakhiyah.

"I think we need to go check on—Cyber. Cyber, Cyber noooo!" Nessiah yelled.

Just as she suspected, Cyber pretended to walk out of the door, but ended up doubling back, she flew across the room like she was Superwoman and landed on top of Aoki's head. Cyber was beating the shit out of the poor girl. Saafiq and Synclaire hopped up and tried to detach the women from each other. Ten minutes, and a whole hand full of weave later, Cyber sat across the room wheezing as her medium sized fingers tightly clutched the chunks of the weave she'd pulled from Aoki's head.

"You know you didn't have to snatch out every piece of shorty's hair, ma," Synclaire said, as he laughed at the memory.

She didn't care about nothing at that moment. She didn't even care about his mother and father giving her displeasing looks. Cyber wasn't one to tolerate disrespect. She had half a mind to go back wherever they were holding her husband and start whooping on his ass for having her show her ass in public, in front of his parents.

⁓

IT WAS GOING ON MIDNIGHT, when she finally felt herself being shaken awake. She instantly sat up and looked around. The only people who were still there was Saafiq, Synclaire and Yakhiyah. Everyone else had left because they were so tired. Turning to face the nurses' station, she saw a short, chubby man in a white coat standing off to the side of her.

"Are you Yakhi Rodriquez's family?"

Cyber jumped to her feet and walked over to the doctor.

"Yes, I am his wife, and these are his brothers and his twin sister," Cyber said, reaching behind herself, trying to get them to step up with her, so they all could hear the status on his condition.

"Mr. Rodriquez is a very lucky man. To have survived the brutal attack is something amazing."

"That's real good shit, G, but is my nigga gon' make it?" Saafiq spoke.

"Yes, sir, your nig—I mean, yes, your brother made it out of surgery successfully. He's getting prepped for recovery and will be in his own private suite very soon. Once he is transferred, I will send his nurse down to get you. In the meantime, please follow me to the recovery waiting room."

Cyber said a silent prayer as she walked the long halls. She was so happy that the Lord spared the love of her life. She decided to let go of all the pain from her past. She just wanted to love on her man and let him love her in return.

14

NESSIAH

The Best Decision, Not The Most Logical One.

"Question my love for you again," he said, as she stared at her name inked neatly on his collarbone.

Nessiah watched in slow motion as he reached into the pocket on his slacks and pulled out a gray square box. He pulled a smaller box out of the larger one and opened the top, revealing a beautiful, rose gold, sixteen-carat, Pink Morganite diamond with fifty-two round, baguette diamonds surrounding the twisted band. Her mind was racing as she stared at the fear in his dark, brown eyes. It seemed as if no one was in the room with the two of them. She couldn't hear a sound besides the beating of her heart. She didn't even notice his mother walking up, until she saw her place a garment bag in his hand.

Her eyes dropped down to the bag in his hand, as he pulled out a beautiful wedding gown. Her eyes bounced all over the intricate, lace details. She couldn't lie and say that the dress wasn't fly, or that he didn't have impeccable taste.

Dominick looked at her for a few seconds, and then without waiting on a response, he dropped down to the floor, sitting on his shins at her feet. She watched in utter amazement as he unzipped the dress, then took her left foot into his hand, he slipped her high-heel off her foot and then slipped her leg into the neck of the dress. After both of her legs were inside the wedding dress, he hiked the dress up her thighs until he reached the top of her thighs.

Feeling the heat and smelling the arousal from her hidden treasure, Dominick leaned forward, placing a delicate kiss on her meaty folds. Looking up at her, he licked his lips before his lips parted.

"I don't need you to answer me, I told you this was forever."

Nessiah was embarrassed that he had done that in front of everyone. In the brief moment of silence, she argued with her heart, as it beat profusely from his sexy attempt to control her decision. Then her mind took control of the situation, shattering not only his heart, but hers as well.

"I'm sorry, but this is where our fairytale ends," she said as she shimmied out of the wedding gown and, placed it into his hands. She then grabbed ahold of Qaseem and quietly left out of the venue.

Nessiah stood at her porcelain island countertop staring down at her engagement ring. The smile that graced her face was a genuine smile. She'd never in her life smiled that wide before; she never had a reason to until now. She knew she would catch a bunch of flack for not doing what everyone expected her to do, and that was the reason why she was so successful in life.

Nessiah always went against the grain. After she matured a little bit, she started making decisions according to what would make her happy. If only it was that simple in her love life. Everyone probably expected her to choose Dominick. Hell, she wanted to choose Dominick too, but she had to look at the bigger picture. If she'd settled for Dominick, would she have been happy? The answer would be no. Now if he didn't have so much baggage that stood about five-eight in stature and 125 pounds, maybe she would've been happy. But he did have that,—her, and she wouldn't be happy if Arlyse was still around.

Her eyes rolled at the mere thought of his fiancée. For the life of her, she couldn't understand how the hell he'd gotten tangled up in that web. That was another reason why she didn't pick him. He lied to her too damn much. He never told her about the little secret arranged marriage. She'd heard about it from a few of Arlyse's family members. He didn't value her enough to tell her the truth. He just expected for her to blindly stand by his side until he was ready to play with her. That wasn't the life she envisioned for herself.

Ring. Ring. Ring.

Looking down at her ringing phone, she noticed it was her assistant, Aoki. She rolled her eyes up in her head. After the little situation at the hospital, she was real cool on Aoki. If it wasn't work related, she didn't want to be bothered. For some reason, she thought that the two of them could be friends. But seeing how she acted in the hospital a few days ago, any thought she could've possibly had about them, and a friendship died when Aoki was getting dragged out of the hospital.

Ring. Ring. Ring.

Another facetime call from Aoki. She blew out a frustrated breath and answered the call.

"Yes, Aoki?" She said as she played with the crumbs on the countertop.

"Dang, what's wrong with you, why you sound so dry?" Aoki asked with annoyance lacing her tone.

"I'm just not in the mood, but what's up?"

"Nothing, I just called to tell you that you had a visitor earlier today," Aoki taunted.

"A visitor, who was it?" Nessiah's face scrunched up as she tried to think of who would be visiting her during the day.

"Oh, it was Mr. Washington." Her voice so nonchalant. Aoki tried to play it cool, but she was slowly starting to hate her boss.

Nessiah had everything that Aoki craved. Everything Nessiah had seemed to come so easily for her, and Aoki was out here scrambling just to get near the path Nessiah took toward being successful. The fact that Dominick was chasing after her when she clearly moved on, burned Aoki up on the inside.

"Dominick?"

"Yes, Mr. Dominick Washington." Aoki said sexily.

"Well, what did he say, why was he looking for me?"

"He didn't say," she said in a flat tone.

"Oh, well it must not have been important then," she said causally.

Nessiah tossed her head back, making the black head band she had on slide off the back of her head. She hadn't seen Dominick since his wedding six and a half months ago, and she wasn't looking forward to seeing him again.

"Yeah, I told him you went to lunch with hubby, and he seemed pretty upset."

"Aoki, why would you tell him that?" Nessiah rolled her eyes.

See, that was the shit she was talking about. She knew damn well how that man felt about her. Hell, she was at the damn wedding, so she knew exactly what went down. So, for the life of her, she couldn't understand why she would tell him that. That was the type of shit that made her want to slap her jealous ass. She had to have been jealous, why else would she tell him that shit?

"Aoki, for future reference, if someone calls or stops by trying to reach me, just take a message. I don't want you telling my whereabouts to anyone, do you understand?"

Aoki pulled the phone away from her ear and stared at the receiver. If Yakhi wasn't in the hospital fighting for his life, she would've given Nessiah a piece of her mind. Instead, she bit her tongue, because she needed her job, especially with Yakhi's tacky, fat ass wife back in the picture.

"Sure thing. And listen, I wasn't trying to be messy. I didn't know you would care about me telling him you went to lunch with Qaseem."

Irritated, Nessiah just wanted to get off the phone at that point, but not before she told her about herself.

"I believe you were trying to be messy. Why? I have no clue. But best believe if the shit happens again, you'll not only be looking for a new nigga to love and support ya ass, but you'll be looking for a new job until you find a nigga to sink your claws into. Have a blessed evening, and I'll see you bright and early on Monday morning," Nessiah said, disconnecting the call.

It was a typical Monday morning. She fought tooth and nail to milk lying in bed for a few more minutes. But after her alarm went off for the fifth time, she decided to get up and get her day started. After a twenty-minute-long shower, Nessiah stood in front of her closet, rubbing shea butter into the crevices of her elbows, as her eyes scanned every piece of fabric in her closet.

She wasn't in the best of moods, so she decided to wear something casual. She pulled the long sleeved, white and light blue, cable knit maxi dress of its hanger and paired it with some long, knee-high, blue jeaned material open-toed stilettos. She smiled as she eyed her light skinned chunky toes. The white toe nail polish really set the shoes off, and ultimately brightened her day just a smidge.

Arriving inside of H.O.P.E, her mood started to sour. She'd temporarily forgotten about the bullshit that Aoki tried to pull. Just the thought of seeing her face made her wish that time would fly by. As she walked off the elevator, she trekked in the direction of her office. She was surprised to see Aoki standing against her door frame, waiting for her with a cup of Chai tea and a box of what she assumed were buttered croissants from the deli down the street.

"Good morning, boss lady, these are for you."

Nessiah stopped in front of her and eyed her from head to toe. She had no desire to argue with her, but she wanted her to know that she was with the shits if need be.

"Don't look like that, I didn't do anything to the food. Just simply a token of apology. I shouldn't have over-stepped my boundaries. I apologize," Aoki said, as she held the food and drink out toward her.

She never spoke a word, as she grabbed the box of pastries and the tea then walked into her office, closing the door behind her. Walking over toward the window, Nessiah dropped the box and the medium sized cup into the trash can. She wasn't eating or drinking shit that she had brought. She would be a damn fool to! Nessiah wasn't even seated in her seat for five minutes, when Aoki buzzed her intercom.

"Boss lady, Ms. James wants to see you in her office in fifteen minutes."

"Good, I got some choice words for that bitch too!" She mumbled to herself.

Nessiah had been waiting to run into Nala again after the whole wedding debacle. The bitch knew what she was doing when she assigned her to plan the rest of Dominick's wedding. Nala knew that Dominick was feeling Nessiah, and she was pissed that he had cut her off for some fat bitch no less. So, she thought she'd give Nessiah a reality check.

NESSIAH PACED BACK and forth as the elevator zoomed up the elevator shaft until it reached the fourth floor. Nessiah impatiently charged at the doors before they could open good. She'd been waiting seven long months to get her hands on Nala, but since she was MIA, she figured she knew that and stayed gone longer on her "little vacation."

Not bothering to knock on the door, she barged into her office and was shocked at the scene before her.

15

NESSIAH

"Sometimes it's not the people who change, it's the mask that falls off." ~Unknown

Sitting in the middle of the room in a black, basic, conference room chair, Dominick sat with Nala's matted ass weave doubled over in his lap, topping him off. Nessiah felt her heart shatter into tiny pieces. She bit the inside of her lip as she watched him enjoying the pleasure, she was blessing his penis with. Clearing her throat, she stood lazily against the door frame as she locked eyes with the man who had stolen her heart, only to tear it into tiny pieces and selfishly trash the dismembered muscle into his pockets, so she couldn't give it to someone else to repair it. She watched as he bit into the flesh on his lip. As Nala's head bobbed up and down like she was trying to win a prize. He kept his eyes locked on hers, giving her the sexiest fuck faces a man of his stature kept hidden from the world. She rolled her eyes, as he clutched her hair tighter, signaling that the end was near.

Deciding not to let him see her up in arms, she masked any leftover feelings she had for him. She held her head high, as she thought about how she dodged the bullet that she was sure would come from loving him. The fatal bullet that could've claimed her life.

"Thank you, God, for a better choice!" she said out loud. "Did you actually want something, or did you call me up here to watch you gargle his children down your throat?"

Nala, totally oblivious to her presence, tried to get up from the floor, but Dominick pulled her back to her knees by her hair.

"Naw, yo' ass ain't fucking done yet. I can still feel the nut swimming in my sack," he said, yanking her mouth down to his crotch.

Nala was embarrassed. She had no idea that Nessiah would show up that soon. She should've known he was up to something when he barged in demanding that she called Nessiah up to her office.

Nessiah walked out of the door and headed back up to her office. As soon as she stepped off the elevator, Aoki was flagging her down. Rolling her eyes, she walked to the threshold of her ·office door, when Aoki handed the receiver to her. Placing the phone to her ear, she heard the hostility in his voice.

"Get ya muthafuckin' ass back up here right now! If

you think I'm playing, let twelve minutes pass and you ain't walking through this door. I'ma come down there and fuck you up in front of everybody."

She tossed the phone onto the desk and walked into her office. Once she was inside, she took off the blazer she had over her dress and sat it down on the back of her chair. She picked up the pencil holder that was full of pens, markers and pencils and threw it across the room. She was so pissed off, she wanted to go back upstairs and fuck him and that bitch up!

She paced back and forth across the carpet until her nerves were calm. She walked over to her desk chair and took a seat. Leaning forward, her forehead found comfort with the top of her desk. She had to constantly tell herself not to cry. Nessiah wanted nothing more than to go blow Dominick's shit out. It wasn't fair that he continued to play with her feelings because he felt like it.

Beep.

"Umm, boss lady, you have company," Aoki whispered into the intercom.

Damn did twelve minutes pass that fast? She questioned, looking over at the clock on the wall.

"Hang the fucking phone up! Nobody told ya cum guzzling ass to tell nobody shit. If you wanna tell on some-damn-body, make sure you tell her how you been throwing the pussy at me. Tell her ass that shit!" Dominick yelled.

The thought to jump up and go lock her door crossed

her mind, but she was too late. He had already barged in, damn near snatching the door off the hinges. She sat up in her chair, trying her best to look unbothered by his and Nala's presence.

"Why the fuck you think I'm always playing with your goofy ass?" He shouted.

Still, she sat back with her fingers interlocked, resting on top of her stomach, just watching as he yelled at her. Her eyes moved over toward her boss, as she stood there looking like she just got done licking nut up off the floor at the movie theatre.

"What is it that I can help you with, Mr. Washington?" She asked casually.

"Yo' Nessiah, stop fucking playing with me, real talk," he said, pointedly.

Sitting up, she leaned forward and clasped her hands together on her desk, as she narrowed her eyes at him.

"Again, what is it that I can help you with, Mr. Washington? Because you're really starting to get on my motherfucking nerves!"

"What the fuck did you tell me the reason was for you being up in my momma's crib?" He asked, grabbing the back of Nala's neck, as she tried to walk out of his reach.

"That Nala assigned me the assignment. Why are you asking me about something that happened seven months ago?"

"Okay, so I'll ask you again, what the fuck was your point of sending her over there?" He shouted in her face.

Nessiah chuckled a little at the sight before her. Nala looked like a little kid that was jacked up by the collar of her blouse, being scolded by her father for stealing a fifty-cent piece of bubble gum from the store.

"I never told her—,"

"So, you still gon' stand here and lie to my fucking face?" He asked, jerking her around.

"Dominick I—"

"Please fix yo' dick suckers to lie again. Please do and see what the fuck happens!"

"I—I did send her over there, but it was only because your mom called and asked me if I knew someone who could help plan the wedding."

"You knew damn well what the fuck you were doing. You did that shit to be fucking messy because I wasn't letting ya smutty ass suck my dick no mo'."

Nessiah sat there and watched the two of them going back and forth. All she wanted to do was get her day started and then ended. She had a date later with Qaseem, and she was excited about that, until dumb and dumber popped up.

"Is it possible for you two to take this up to her office and argue about some shit that happened seven months ago?"

"Because it's about respect. This bitch stood there and lied to my muthafuckin' face. And she knows I don't take disrespect lightly."

"What fucking difference did it make? You mad at me

because of what? Your mother asked me for a favor and I—,"

"I don't care what the fuck she asked. You could've sent another fucking person to do the shit, but you sent her thinking that she didn't know about Arlyse, and she already fucking knew."

"But did she know that you were still fucking me too?" Nala sassed.

A flash of horror covered her face, as she watched him literally slap spit from her mouth. With her hands to her mouth, Nessiah jumped to her feet and rushed over toward him. She ran up on him and started hitting him. It was true, she couldn't stand the ground Nala walked on, especially after the whole wedding incident, but that didn't mean she deserved for his overly grown, gotta-have-his-cake-and-eat-it-too ass to hit her because she aired out all his business.

"Are you fucking crazy?" She yelled as she punched him in his ribcage.

Did he think that seeing Nala sucking his dick wouldn't give her the impression that they were sleeping together? She wondered. Dominick hadn't been the topic of discussion between her and her conscience for quite sometime, and seeing him triggered some old emotions. That was until she saw him beating up on her boss.

"Yo' what the fuck you hitting me for?"

"Are you serious right now?"

"Yo', you bugging the fuck out right now. You fighting me, while I'm trying—,"

"No, motherfucker! You bugging hitting on her like that. The fuck is wrong with you?"

"She tried to ruin what the fuck we were building. I don't tolerate disrespect. Period," he said, hoovering over her.

Funny how he was so bold to hit Nala but wouldn't lift his hand up to swat Nessiah. Queens demand respect, remember that!

"So, you think the answer is putting your fucking hands on her? So, what if I do something to piss you off, you gone hit me too?" She asked with her arms crossed over her chest.

Dominick blacked out. Just hearing Nala's excuse for ruining his chance with Nessiah sent him into a blind rage, and he snapped. Standing there looking at the disgusted look that Nessiah was giving him, had him tucking his tail in defeat. He knew he had officially fucked up any chance with her.

"Baby—baby, cum'mere. I fucked up, I know, but let me make it right. Please?" He asked as he reached out toward her.

"You need to apologize to Nala and then you need to leave and never contact me again," she said, moving away from him.

"Nessiah."

Growing frustrated, she waved her hands in the air wildly. She just really wanted him up out of her space.

"Just go, Dominick." She made her way back behind her desk, as her eyes stayed trained on him.

"Can you just give me a fucking minute to explain? Baby, there ain't shit in this world that you could do to me to make me put my hands on you," he said as he started moving toward her.

He felt like he was inside of a vacuumed sealed tube. He couldn't breath and he was dying to be next to her. He was craving to just be in her space, breathing the same air as her.

"Dominick, please leave before I call the police."

His eyes widened and then they narrowed. He couldn't believe she'd threatened to call twelve on him. The last thing he wanted to do was make her scared of him. When he hesitated to move, she picked up the receiver from its cradle and started to dial the emergency number.

"A'ight,—a'ight, I'll go. You can hang up the phone, bae."

When she didn't make a move to place the phone down, he knew she was seriously not fucking with him. He walked over toward the door and opened it. With his body half-way out the door, he paused and stood still for a few moments. He finally walked out of the door, closing it quietly behind him. Nessiah, tired from the mess, grabbed her cellphone and shot Qaseem a text.

Nessiah: *I need a rain check.* 😩

QA: *Is everything alright?*

Nessiah: *Something like that,—I'm just really tired, ttyl.*

QA: *Do you want me to stop by later?*

Nessiah read the message and put her phone away. Her head lifted up and she saw Nala standing in the same spot as before, caressing her bruised cheek. The silence was deafening, both caught up in their thoughts and feelings.

"I guess I had you pegged all wrong. I—I'm sorry, Nessiah, I truly am. And thank you for sticking up for me, when you clearly didn't have to."

"Close my door on your way out, Nala. And while you're at it, thank the good Lord it was him that slapped you and not me," she said, wiping her tongue over her teeth.

Well, I did say that I wanted the time to fly by.

16

SAAFIQ

Been A Minute Since You Called Me

Passed white boy wasted, Saafiq sat in the front seat of his 2018 pearl Yukon. He sniffed another line of the zannie bar he'd just crushed up. His life had started to spiral downhill since Yakhiyah decided to stop fucking with him. A lot of people think that it's a choice to do this or that, which is partially true, but not completely. It's like before you find something to live for, something or someone to do right by, you don't care about the reckless shit that you do. But then you find that something or someone that gives you purpose and you suddenly find yourself wanting or needing to do better. Then once you don't have that thing or person, you go back to not giving a fuck about wanting to do right. And that's exactly how Saafiq felt. He knew that waiting too long to get his shit together was going to fuck him up in the end, but he ignored that fact and figured he'd cross that bridge when he got to it.

Sniffing the last line, he threw his head back and closed his eyes tightly. He used the palm of his hand to rub his nose obnoxiously, until the tingling sensation subsided.

"Why are you parked outside of my house?" She said from outside his window.

He bit his bottom lip. He wasn't expecting her to up this early in the morning. He suddenly sat up straight, trying to get himself together. If he'd known that she was up, he wouldn't have snorted those last two lines. He swallowed hard as the thought of her seeing him high crossed his mind. Yakhiyah pounded on the glass with her fist.

"Why the fuck are you out here this early in the morning?" She stood there covered in a pink, Terry cloth robe and some white bunny slippers.

"Saafiq!" She screamed.

Tired of her causing a scene, he leaned over and rolled down the window.

"Why yo' ass out here making all that damn noise?" He said with his eyes closed. He felt like his head was floating in a tank full of water.

"No, the real question is why the hell are you parked outside my house? stalking me and shit? That's what I want to know."

"You my bitch, so how the fuck is that considered stalking?" He asked as he leaned over toward the window, eyes plastered on her beautiful bare face, totally forgetting that he was high off narcotics instead of her presence.

"Are you high again?"

He leaned back against the seat after he realized he was busted.

"Fuck you mean again?" He said, picking up the hat that sat next to him on the passenger seat, placing it on his head so low that the brim shielded his befuddled eyes.

"Again, as in this is the second time, I've seen your fucking pupils dilated and bugged outta your fucking skull, Saafiq."

He waved her off, as he closed his eyes again.

"What the fuck did you take?" She asked, yanking on the car door handle.

"Yo', you bugging. Stop before you tear my shit up, he said, unbothered by her concern.

"What the fuck was it, coke?"

His eyes popped open that time. "Fuck naw! I ain't no fucking base head. Watch out, shawty," he said, slapping her hands off the window.

"You might as well be. What the fuck did you take, Saa?"

"I'm just tired, I ain't get no sleep last night."

"I bet, ya ass too busy watching my every move. Now what did you take?"

"I ain't take shit, man, chill out."

"Open the door," she said, yanking on the door handle.

"For what?" He asked, looking over at her.

"Because I wanna see what the fuck is in your truck." She reached over the glass and tried to pull the lock up with her fingers.

"What the fuck you gone do, pump my stomach or some shit?" He asked as he laughed.

"So, you ingested something? What was it, shrooms?"

"Ya-Ya, chill out."

"No! Why the fuck would you come to my shit high? Fuck kinda shit you on?"

"Why the fuck you out here making a fucking scene? Take ya ass back in the fucking house with all that fake love," He said dismissively.

Climbing up on the lift on his truck, she reached through the window and started slapping him in the face. The hits were coming so fast, and with him being high, his reaction time was delayed. All he could do was push her arms out the way. Not liking the fact that he felt like she was trying to punk him, he opened the car door, and got out.

"The fuck is your problem, B?"

"Get the fuck out of my face, Saa," she said, shoving him in the chest.

"Naw, talk all that reckless shit now, shawty," he said, invading her space.

"Fuck outta here, you stupid ass junky. Don't talk outta the side of your fucking face to me because when I tried to show you that I was riding for you, you walked the fuck away!" She yelled.

Hearing her call, him a junky pissed him off. He bit down on his inner jaw, to keep from hitting her.

"Watch ya fucking dick suckers, shawty."

"Don't worry about who's dick I'm sucking. Just know it ain't yours. Ya little ass shit probably won't even get the fuck up, with as much coke ya ass tootin'," she said, turning to walk toward her front porch.

Walking up behind her, he snatched her up by the back of her robe and lifted her feet off the ground, carrying her into the house.

"Saa, put me the fuck down, I'm not playing!"

Walking further into the living room, he tossed her on the couch, as he unbuckled his pants.

Yakhiyah sat up and watched as his rock-hard penis popped out of the slit in the front of his boxers. She had to bite her bottom lip to keep the drool inside her mouth.

"Come over here," he motioned.

Her eyes stayed glued to the glob of precum that was oozing from his bulbous head. She could feel the goose bumps as they slowly crept up the inside of her thighs. The feeling was so intense, she almost opened her legs, forgetting she didn't have any panties on.

"Come see if this coked out dick can still have ya thick ass running from him," he said. Standing to his feet, he slid his gray jogging pants down his toned thighs, until they stopped and slouched at his ankles.

Yakhiyah turned her head, not wanting to fall victim to his tempting offer. It had been way too long for him to be playing dick games, like she wouldn't say fuck celibacy and rape his sexy ass.

Saafiq kicked his shoes off his feet and then moved into her line of vision. Her big, doe shaped, brown eyes trailed from his thick calves, up to his muscular hips, bouncing up to his tight, tatted abdomen and finally to his beautiful face. His thick hair was curly and hanging under the sides of his hat, covering his shaven sides. His eyes were low from the drugs, but they gave off a seductive stare. Yakhiyah silently prayed for the strength to hold on to her pledge. Saafiq grabbed the base of his dick and rubbed the tip along the bottom of her jaw line. Fighting the urge to turn her head, so he could put it in her mouth, she stood to her feet. She tried to walk away from temptation, but he caught her by the waist. Snaking his long arms around her, he pulled her into his side.

"Why you running, shawty? Don't run from me, run towards me," he said as he nipped at the nape of her neck.

His hands slowly crept down her side and in between her thighs. He had to hold on to her as her knees buckled. She was trying so hard not to give into his enticement, but it was hard fighting love head up. No matter how many times she told herself that she wasn't fucking with Saafiq anymore, she knew the real once they were face to face with each other.

"Saa, don't do this, please. I've been doing so good, please—ooohhhh Godddd," she moaned.

With his index finger, he parted her puffy lips and used his middle finger to crack open Pandora's box.

"I need you! How you gon' deny me of what's mine?" He moaned.

His fingers pumped vigorously inside of her wet walls.

"You not playing fair," she whined.

"Ain't nothing fair about my love for you," he said, moaning in her ear. Saafiq used the tip of his tongue to trace the outside of her ear.

"Please, daddy."

"Please what, Ya-Ya? Tell daddy what you want."

She was so wet, you could hear her pussy gushing like the falls of Niagara from the next room.

"Saa, I'm 'bout to come," she whispered.

"No, you not!"

"Yes, I am, baby."

"Oh, yeah? A'ight, tell me when you 'bout to come, shawty, so I can catch all of that shit!"

"Saa...,"

"You coming, beautiful?"

"Yyyeess."

"A'ight coo," he said, pulling his finger from out of her vagina and stuffing them into his warm mouth.

"Nooooo, Saafiq, stop playing for real!" She said as she reached for him.

He said nothing as he moved to the other side of the room, where he stood pulling his pants back up. He wanted to fuck her so bad, but she'd bruised his ego. Now he wasn't fucking with her like that.

"Oh, I know ya ass don't think you about to go some-where." She watched with a bewildered look on her face.

Still, he said nothing, as he slipped his Balenciaga's on his feet and trekked toward the front door.

"Saafiq, I'm like dead ass serious. I wanna come," she whined.

Opening the door, he didn't even look back, as he walked out and slammed it behind him.

I bet she wished she wouldn't have insulted this little coked out dick now!

He chuckled to himself, as he climbed into his truck.

17

AOKI

Eyes on The Prize

Who said that a woman couldn't have everything she desired for herself? What if everything she desired belonged to someone else? That was the story of Aoki Lee's life. Aoki was known as a woman who fought tooth and nail to get whatever she wanted. It didn't matter what it was; from jobs to bags all the way down to someone else's man. She always had a hustler's mentality; get it by any means necessary.

That was a rare trait today. So many people felt like they were owed something, always walking around with their hands out, begging. That wasn't Aoki though. She didn't care what she had to do to accomplish one of her goals. She wasn't above kneeling for hours if it meant she would get the prize at the end. She was what most would call conniving or crafty. At the moment, Aoki had her eyes

set on two very different projects that demanded her attention. The last project titled *Get Dominick Washington* was
put on hold when she met Yakhi Rodriquez, but seeing his
undying love for her boss, Nessiah, she couldn't scrap her
original plan. Aoki wanted,—no, needed both Yakhi and
Dominick. Just thinking about the power both men
possessed made her pussy cream the heaviest orgasm
known to man.

Then there was Yakhi's out of the blue 'wifey'. She was
seeing red when the fat ass bitch popped up at the day
party a few weeks ago. At first, she didn't pay the woman
any attention, but when she noticed that Yakhi was staring
the woman all up-side the head, she sat back and watched
his sneaky ass a little more closely. Then the bitch called
herself introducing herself, and flashed the biggest rock
she'd ever seen, sitting pretty on her little fat ass fingers.

Yakhi didn't make the situation any better, as he openly
stared at her while, she walked around the party mingling
with the other guest. Aoki was pissed. She wanted to look
around and see if she saw some emergency sponsors in the
party but couldn't because she didn't want to give his wife
the chance to be all up in his face.

So, together they sat—well, she sat back and watched
him watch her. Aoki was a very selfish and jealous person.
If it wasn't all about her then she had a problem and the
problem was YOU! She felt she was entitled to whatever
she wanted, and unfortunately, those around her encour-
aged her difficult mindset.

She sat at her desk, as she waited to go and 'check on' Nessiah. She was listening intently as her, Dominick and Nala argued back and forth about how she set Nessiah up, by sending her to plan Dominick's wedding with his mother. She thought the plan that Nala had come up with was clever, but she felt she could've executed it way better, and wouldn't gotten caught.

She had to keep telling herself to tread lightly when it came to Nessiah. When she first started filling in for Nessiah's previous secretary, she got the vibe that she was the push over type. Anyone with two working eyes could sense that she wasn't the most confident person. So, Aoki thought she had it in the bag. Her thinking that she was going to come in and sweep Dominick off his feet, was her first mistake. She had totally underestimated Nessiah and what she was capable of. When Nessiah checked her over the phone, she couldn't lie and pretend that she hadn't rattled her nerves a bit. So, she told herself to try and befriend her again, then slowly execute her plan while appearing to be the caring friend. But what Aoki didn't know was that Nessiah had no plans of ever being her friend, and she was keeping her at arm's length with both eyes open.

Her ears perked up when she heard the doorknob turn, and out stormed Dominick with the meanest mug on his face.

"Excuse me, Mr. Washington," she said as she cleared her throat.

"What?" He said in the meanest tone she'd ever heard.

"I was just making sure you were okay," she said, appearing very sensitive.

"I'll hit you up later when I want my dick sucked. And the shit better be superb as thirsty as your tact headed ass is." He tossed over his shoulder as his tall frame entered the elevator.

Aoki sat there with her mouth wide open. She didn't know if she should've been offended or turned on. She was definitely turned on, as her hands brushed across her hardened pink nipples.

She was so excited that she could hardly sit still in her seat. She was going to use this opportunity to wow him and secure her place in his life by any means. Just the thought of having him all to herself and spending all his money he'd accumulated standing on the corners hustling had her rummaging through her drawers, looking for her hot pink bullet disguised in a black M.A.C lipstick tube.

After she found what she was looking for, she rushed off to the bathroom to rid herself of the nagging nut that was slowly building in anticipation of feeling his swollen shaft busting her open from asshole to appetite. Flying inside the stall, she hiked her pencil skirt up to her waist. She unscrewed the tube, turned the vibrator on its highest setting and applied it to her hardened clitoris.

As the waves of vibrations flowed through the tip to her sensitive pearl tongue, she thanked God for the creation and giving her the thought not to wear any panties. Aoki stayed in the bathroom stall pleasuring herself on company time with thoughts of Dominick sending her off into the clouds.

"Now I just need to bring my A-game to hook his ass. First things first, my ass is going home to douche with some hot ass water and vinegar." she thought to herself.

18

DOMINICK

Cursed!

It was several hours after the photoshoot for Figure 8, and Dominick was on a high no one could bring down. He felt truly blessed that he was able to bring so many talented people in on his project and pull it off. After the shoot, he took everyone out for dinner and drinks, for their contribution to aiding in his dream coming true.

It wasn't until hours later, that he found himself pinned against the large, glass window with his head tossed back. He tried to relax and enjoy the pleasure that was radiating through his body, compliments of her warm and moist mouth. He knew that he was foul for having his dick shoved pass Aoki's tonsils, but shit, she was offering, and it wasn't like he was getting head at home or from Nessiah.

Even though he told himself that he wasn't doing shit

wrong because she had a whole fiancé at home, he couldn't help but feel like he was cheating on Nessiah. Dominick knew that women analyzed things differently. They automatically assumed that if her nigga was giving the dick away, he was attracted to the side bitch, when sometimes that's just not the case. It definitely wasn't his case. Aoki was just something to do because he couldn't do who he wanted to do. She was far from his type. He liked his women overly thick and non-dehydrated. He honestly thought that if he was fucking off, he would be able to rid his mind of her, but it only made the situation worse.

Instead of him enjoying the wetness that coated his thick, veiny shaft, he was worried about if she was topping her fiancé off, or if, with the proper guidance, she could blow a head hunter like Aoki out of the water.

"What's the matter?" She asked as her head popped up from between his legs.

He looked down and noticed that the swelling in his penis had went down. He shook his head and stood to his feet. Just as she was about to question him again, his office door flew open. Nessiah stood in the doorway with Dani not too far behind her.

"I tried to tell her that you were busy," Dani said, peeking over her shoulder.

Quickly he shoved his penis into his underwear and buckled his belt. He bit down on the inside of his jaw, thinking that his momma should've named him 'can't get right', because he just couldn't seem to catch a break or do right in her eyes.

Aoki was totally caught off guard and it showed as the three of them watched her try to ease underneath the desk. With the look Nessiah had on her face, she wasn't sure what the hell was about to happen, but she knew she didn't want to be on the receiving end of it.

"There's no need for you to try and hide, I've already seen ya tact-headed, dehydrated ass. Ain't you dating my friend's twin brother?" She questioned, as the thought had just hit her.

No one said anything, everyone just stood there looking at each other. Nessiah gave him one last look and walked away.

"Nessiah."

She kept walking as she ignored his cat calls. Just reaching the outside door, her arm was snatched backward.

"Dominick, get your fucking hands off me."

"No, not until you talk to me," he said in a frustrated breath.

"There's nothing to talk about. I just dropped by to—,"

"You dropped by for what?"

Nessiah stopped and just gazed out the front door. She didn't know why she was there. One minute she was sitting in her office watching the hustle and bustle that Downtown Detroit was known for, and the next, she was pulling up outside his office.

"I stopped by to congratulate you on a job well done with Figure 8. I don't know why I wasted my time, though, shit with you will never change! Let go of my arm and get back to what you were doing." She spoke lowly as she tried to free her arm from his grasp.

"You know damn well that's not the reason why you stopped by. We both know why, so stop playing fucking games, Nessiah. I'm right here, just say the word and I'm all yours."

"Mine and how many other bitches is in the fucking cult?" She turned and looked at him.

"Siah, knock it the fuck off. You know damn well it's always been you. From the moment I first met you, I showed interest in you. You were a breath of fresh air for me, in your own unfashionable way. But that was part of the reason I fell for you. You not out here trying to be like the rest of these birds. Your sense of style and overall personality is unique. That's what attracted me to you."

"Let go of my arm, Dominick." She was annoyed that she even came there. She didn't want him thinking that she was dumb and gullible just to be in his presence.

"Stop that shit! You're overthinking the shit. Just give me the opportunity to show you that you're all I want—all I need," he stated, kissing the back of her hand. That innocent gesture had a heat wave rushing from her bright yellow cheeks down below to the deepest part of her love.

"I can't hurt Qa like that. That wouldn't be fair to him, Dominick." She turned her head, refusing to look at him.

"Fuck that nigga! What about me, huh?" he said, snatching her into his embrace forcibly.

He was at his wits end with her defiant attitude. She just wouldn't go with the flow, and he needed her to. He wasn't trying to be the type of dude to have her looking dumb in these Detroit streets. Dominick really had all the intentions in the world to do right by Nessiah. He wanted to show her unconditional love. He wanted to be there for the step-by-step process of her learning to love herself. He wanted to be her everything, but she wasn't feeling it.

"You keep making this all about you. What about your fucking feelings? You have a whole fiancée at home, yet you're here with your penis stuffed down my secretaries throat!" She barked.

"That bitch doesn't mean shit to me, beautiful. Simply something to do until you come around."

"Yeah, and I guess I mean something to you, huh?"

"You damn right you do. But you knew that already, you dead ass just want me to say it."

"I don't want you to say a fucking word. It's your actions I pay attention to, and this—," she said waving her hand around, speaking on the environment where they stood.

"This shows me that you're not ready to be exclusive with me. That's all I need, Dominick, that's all I've ever wanted; someone who wants me for me."

"Baby, I do though. I been about you since day one. What, you think I'm going this hard behind some pussy?

Ma, I dead ass haven't even been on no shit like that wit' chu, and you know it."

"I just can't, seriously. Qaseem would never have me out here looking foolish like this. Like, why is it that you think you marrying someone else and trying to have me on the side is cool?"

"For the last fucking time, IT'S BUSINESS!" He hissed.

"Oh yeah, this mysterious business deal you got going on with her. Yeah, I forgot all about your little arranged marriage bullshit."

He ran his hand over his face in defeat. He was tired! It didn't matter what the situation was about, she was going to continue to fight him. If he was being serious with himself, the whole situation was draining all the energy, he had left inside of him. Dominick sat down in the middle of the floor. He was thankful that it was after hours, because the floor where his office was located is always busy buzzing with people walking back and forth from their cubicles to the elevators.

He leaned his head forward, on his forearm, with both of his hands attached an inch above his wrists. His legs supported his arms and they rested tautly on his knee caps. He was taking deep breaths as he tried to focus on what he was about to say. Over the course of those seven months without Nessiah, he had found himself doing things he never thought that he would do. Chasing after any woman was high up on that list of don'ts.

If she couldn't trust in him, there was really no point in

begging, her to give him another chance. Another item on his don't list. Nessiah wasn't totally to blame for the fallout; he had to assume 95% of the blame. It was his doing that lead her not to trust him anymore, so he had to man up and handle his business.

"You know what? You're absolutely right! I fucked up and I can't expect you to welcome me back in with open arms, especially when the shit between us was so new. I'll have to live with my fucked up choices for the rest of my life." His eyes dropped down as he felt the stinging sensation penetrating the back of his Cornea.

"Just do me a favor, don't let up on that nigga. Make his ass earn everything you have to offer, darling."

And with that, he stood to his feet and turned his back on Nessiah, heading back to his office. For once, he wasn't going to be selfish. He had fucked with that girl's feelings time and time again. Now he was going to set her free so that she could experience true happiness. Even if the thought did kill him.

19

NESSIAH

The One I Gave My Heart To

She must've stood there for half an hour trying to gain clarity from his words. Her heart thumped with a tremendous amount of force. She couldn't believe that he'd given up. She didn't know what to expect. On one hand, she was pissed off that he walked away so easily. To her, if he could walk away like it didn't affect him, then the feelings weren't genuine from the get-go. And then she was happy that he was being selfless. She was torn between what was right and what her heart wanted. Nessiah knew she had no business putting herself in a situation like that.

Not only was the situation embarrassing, but how could she possibly take Dominick home to her family? What—or better yet, how would she have explained their relationship? This generation was so social media crazy, that at any moment, Arlyse could post something on Face

Book, Snap Chat, IG or Twitter, and someone she knows could easily tag her in the status or go back and tell her mother and father. Nessiah was friends with a lot of her relatives and people from her old neighborhood, so it would be nothing for them to see when she was tagged in anything negative.

Eventually she left, once she realized that he was serious and not coming back for her. Maybe it was for the best! She did have Qaseem after all, and he had been a damn good fiancé to her. She leaned her head against the steering wheel as she pouted. She just wished that Dominick would've gotten his shit together before it was too late for them.

SEVERAL WEEKS HAD PASSED and Nessiah was doing everything she could to keep her mind focused on all the things she needed to get done before her wedding day. Between secretly working on the launch of Figure 8's Spring collection and other projects for H.O.P.E, planning her wedding and being attentive to Qaseem, she was worn out. Yes, she was still working with Aoki behind the scenes to launch F8's clothing line. Dominick had the photoshoot a few weeks prior, and with some additions and subtractions, the shoot was *finally* a success.

Dominick had really shocked Nessiah. He was being a man of his word by keeping his distance. He even sent her an e-mail formally apologizing for any "miscommunication" and relieved her of her duties as plus sized model number four. In the beginning, she fought him on doing the shoot, but once he cited that it would be a conflict of interest, she felt sad, about the missed opportunity.

Nessiah had begun working with Cyber and Yakhiyah for the photoshoot, while collaborating for his event, they had all gotten close and made sure to meet up for breakfast every Saturday morning, and they were gym buddies on Mondays and Thursdays. Being the only child, she never knew how much fun it was to have "siblings," even if they weren't blood related. They told each other everything and laughed and had fun like they'd known each other all their lives instead of almost a full year.

It was five-thirty in the evening and Nessiah, Cyber, Yakhiyah and Delores, Nessiah's wedding planner, were all sitting in the den area in Cyber's house going over the seating arrangements for her wedding, when they finally decided to call it quits. Delores packed up her stuff and headed out, and Nessiah felt like she could finally breathe. All the wedding talk and then her overwhelming thoughts about Dominick had her ready to explode. She had been waiting all day to get some alone time with her sisters because she really needed to vent. She had no one else to talk to and knew they wouldn't judge her. Well, she hoped they wouldn't!

"So, I have something to tell you guys," Nessiah said as she fiddled with her fingers.

The girls stopped messing around with floral arrangements and the seating charts, giving her their undivided attention.

"I—I don't want you to judge me, but I can't keep this secret bottled up another day."

"You know we would never judge you! We are sisters and we're here for you, whenever you need us," Yakhiyah said, rubbing her back.

"What the hell is it? You ain't dying, are you?" Cyber blurted out.

No, I'm not—,"

"Owwee, bitch, you gay, ain't chu?" Cyber said in an animated voice, with her eyes squinted.

"What? Hell, no, I'm not gay. Why the hell would you ask me that shit?"

"I don't know, you were checking me out a few weeks ago." She shrugged her shoulders.

"Bitch, I gave ya pregnant ass a compliment, and now you think I'm gay?" Nessiah shook her head and then focused her attention on Hiyah. "I—I've been under a lot of stress with planning this wedding and all and then—,"

"Aht, aht! Bitch, please don't tell me you gon' ditch that man at the altar."

"Cyber, stop cutting the damn girl off, Jesus. Now what were you saying?"

Inhaling a sharp breath, Nessiah counted to ten in her head and then everything that she had planned for the weekend came spewing out her mouth like word vomit.

"I've been in my feelings about the whole Dominick situation, so I canceled dinner with Qa this weekend and I rented a room downtown. I stopped at the mall yesterday and brought some smell good candles from Bath and Body Works, and I even picked up some lingerie from Torrid. After my trip to the mall, I went to the room and started setting up, so that everything will be perfect. I've already typed up the text I'm going to send Dominick. I'm going to give him my umm....,"

"Bitch, just spit it the fuck out damn!" Yakhiyah screamed.

"I'm giving him my virginity." She said, breaking eye contact.

"You givin' who your virginity?" Cyber hopped off the couch as fast as her seven-month belly would allow.

"I'm going to let Dominick take my virginity."

"Oh God! Come on now, Nessiah, what are you thinking about?"

"I'm thinking that I just wanted to enjoy myself and step outside of the box before I sign my life over to Qaseem."

"You said that like it's a death sentence," Cyber interjected.

"Well, I didn't mean it like that, Cyber, and could you please stop looking at me with the judgmental glare?"

"I'm not giving you a judgmental glare, I just can't believe my ears," she said, shaking her head back and forth.

"What brought on this sudden, rash decision, Nessiah?" Yakhiyah asked.

Nessiah sat back against the couch and tossed her head back, eyes closed as she tried to envision every possible way she could bring him and herself pleasure, if she was to go through with her secret rendezvous.

"Well, I was up in my bedroom doing research for HOPE's new market strategy meeting and an ad from XNXX popped up on the screen. Curious, I clicked the ad and watched a couple videos."

She remembered her emotions were running high at the time. Several times she asked herself if it was something she could go through with, since the idea popped in her head. She wasn't a heartless bitch, she cared about Qaseem very much. She was falling for him in the worst way, but she had to have a selfish moment, so she wouldn't regret her decision in the long run. She closed her eyes tight, envisioning every single detail that helped her made a consensus decision.

"I know you guys think that this idea is the stupidest thing you've ever heard, but I have to do this for me. Y'all have had several encounters with men, you both know what it feels like to be desired by a man. You know what it feels like to have a man stare at you with a look that says he wants to rip your clothes off with his teeth. I've never experienced that!" She said on the verge of tears.

"Okay, so why not lose your virginity to your fiancé?" Yakhiyah asked.

"Qaseem is old fashioned. He wants to do things the right way and wait until we're married. Besides, I want to do it with Dominick. He gives me all of those feelings. He makes me feel desirable and sexy."

Cyber and Yakhiyah sat there and listened intently to her vent. They had really grown to love Nessiah like a sister. They weren't going to sit there and judge her because she consciously decided to put her happiness first. Yeah, what she was planning to do was wrong as hell, especially to Qaseem, because he was trying so hard to make her fall in love with him. But sometimes we are allotted a time or two to be completely selfish. Her planning to sleep with Dominick was selfish, but it would also allow her to close the door on that chapter in her life.

"It's not my intention to hurt Qa, but I need to be sure that I'm choosing him for all the right reasons."

"So, how exact is this supposed to work? What if Qa calls looking for you?"

"I'm going to tell him that I want to be alone, and I'll call him first thing in the morning. Qa is a creature of habit, so he'll probably be in the bed before ten-thirty."

THAT WEEKEND CAME FASTER than Nessiah expected it to. Just like she had told her friends, the room she reserved for her first night, was set up with all the amenities that a girl could only dream of. She decorated the room in dark reds and burgundies, and she had rose petals, champagne and chocolates. One might've thought that she was over doing it with the ambiance, but she wanted her first time to be special, even if it was wrong by some's standards.

Nessiah showered and oiled her body down with peach mango shea butter. When she was finished, she slipped on the burgundy teddy she purchased from Torrid. She sat at the table in front of the mirror and applied mascara and lip gloss to her face. She didn't want to put on any make-up and risk ruining the mood, because his overly cocky ass had an issue with her wearing makeup.

When she was satisfied with her natural look, she took off her bonnet and combed her bone straight hair down from the wrap she had it in. She smiled as she eyed the fresh silk press she'd gotten earlier in the day. Her nerves started to get the best of her, as she grabbed her cell phone and looked down at the pre-typed message to Dominick. She took a couple of deep breaths and then pressed send. Ten minutes passed, and she started to worry. When she texted him in the past, she never had to wait for a response.

"Maybe he blocked my number," she mumbled to herself.

Beep.

Her eyes dropped down to the screen on her cellphone. Seeing his name scroll across the screen, her stomach tightened.

Dominick: What kind of shit you on?

Nessiah: *What do you mean?*

Dominick: *Yo' who the fuck is this?*

Nessiah: *Nessiah, who else would it be?*

Confused, her eyebrows furrowed. If she wasn't already looking at his name in the middle of her screen, she would've doubled check to make sure she'd texted the right person.

Ring. Ring. Ring.

Her nerves twitched every second her phone vibrated across the table. She wasn't expecting him to call her, but what was the point of being scared to talk to him over the phone, if she would have to see him when he showed up?

"Hello?"

"Repeat what you just texted me."

"Dominick, I sent the text. Are you coming over to talk or not?"

"Not! I'm busy, and I'm not in the mood to talk about Figure 8."

"Why, are you with another woman?"

"Not that it's any of your business, no, I'm not, and I still don't feel like talking about—,"

"I lied. I texted you because I want you to take my virginity," she said quickly.

The line had gone silent. Nessiah held her breath as she waited for him to respond.

"Run that pass me again," he said quietly.

"Don't make me repeat myself," she groaned.

"Naw, you gon' have to. I need to know I'm not hallucinating or some shit."

"I want you to take my virginity," she whispered into the receiver.

Again, he was quiet on the other end. So many thoughts were running through his mind. He didn't know what to say. Well, he did, he just didn't want to turn her down.

"I can't."

"Why not?" Instantly, her mind started making up excuses as to why he didn't want her like that. She bit down on her lip to keep the tears from falling.

"Nessiah, let's be real, you can't even say the shit out loud over the phone. And then I don't want you to regret giving me a piece of you later."

"But I won't regret it. Look, if you don't want to do it because of how I look and my weight, just say that. You don't have to make up excuses to not—,"

"Where you at?" He said, cutting her off.

Her eyes darted up to the mirror, as she watched herself talk into the receiver.

"I'm at Greektown, room 1024," she said.

A COUPLE DAYS had passed since "operation rid herself of her present" had taken place and surprisingly, she didn't feel anything. She thought she would've felt guilty, but she didn't. Nessiah walked around JoAnn fabrics with Yakhiyah and Cyber, talking about what happened that night.

"Okay, I'm officially confused," Yakhiyah said, swiping her bangs from her face.

"It was a mistake because Qa didn't deserve that and furthermore, I never should've done it, because it's going to be super hard giving up all of that caramel," she said, wiping her hand down her mouth, in a way that suggested she was trying to erase the words that left her pink painted lips.

"You don't feel bad for doing it, but you feel bad that you did it while you're engaged to Qaseem?"

"Exactly," she mumbled. When she said it in her head, it made sense. But once she vocalized it to someone else who wasn't in her shoes, it sounded crazy as hell!

"So, what are you going to do about your wedding?" Cyber asked.

"I'm still getting married. I owe him that. I—I would never play with his feelings like that," Nessiah said as a sigh left her sticky lips.

"But are you getting married for yourself, or are you doing it to soothe your guilty conscience? And don't think I didn't notice that you didn't tell me all the juicy deets," Cyber said, as she rolled her eyes.

"Doesn't matter the reason, I'm getting married to Qaseem Lord Maten. And I purposely didn't go into detail. Somethings are better left unsaid. Just know that it was a magical mistake, end of discussion." She walked away, headed to the check-out counter with an arm full of different colored rolls of fabrics.

Sometimes you must sacrifice your wants and needs to make others happy.

20

YAKHI

IT'S THE LITTLE THINGS THAT MATTERS MOST

Have you ever felt like you were floating on thin air, with water clogging your ears? Or what about going swimming, taking a shower or washing your hair; and the water gets into your ears then you temporarily can't hear clearly? That was what Yakhi had experienced while he was out. He didn't even know that he was in a coma until he could finally hear clearly.

Yakhi didn't even know subconsciously the details of what had happened to him. He was disorientated. He could hear the voices, but they weren't clear to the point where he could make out who it was and what they were saying. All that bullshit they try to make you believe about dying, your life flashing before your eyes and see the bright white lights, is a crock of bullshit fabricated for the television shows.

When he finally had the strength to open his eyes, he

was all alone. His eyes bounced off the white walls as he tried to figure out where he was. In between the doctors and nurses running in and out of his room, he couldn't get much sleep, so he stared out the window, watching as the sky turned from bright blue to pitch black. One of the nurses that was too eager to ride his limp dick told him how he ended up in the hospital.

The next day rolled around, and he was still just as lost as the previous day. He had so many questions, and he was getting frustrated because everyone around him pretended like they didn't know how or who had shot him three times. All that changed as soon as Aoki showed up. She basically pumped his head up, telling him that it was Layah and even insinuated that Cyber was in cahoots with the whole plan.

Yakhi was so pissed off at the things Aoki was telling him. To make matters worse, Cyber hadn't shown up to see him. Aoki told him lie after lie, and he ate it all up and ran with it. Yakhi kind of felt bad that he hadn't given her a fair chance to get to know him. He lay slouched in the bed as he watched her cleaning up his room. Just watching how attentive she was, is what made him decide to give their relationship a fair chance. He couldn't wait until he was feeling better so that he could go out combing the streets looking for Layah. Once he found her, he was going to find Cyber next and make her watch him kill the bitch who almost killed him.

As a reflex, his fist balled up underneath the covers and

a mug covered his face. Just thinking of how disloyal her fat ass was had his skin hot. He couldn't even be mad at her for real because he was the one who pursued her. She told him repeatedly that she would never give up pussy, but he was too stupid to think he could flip her.

"Baby, what's wrong?" Aoki asked, turning around, noticing the tensed look on his face.

Yakhi was so zoned out into his thoughts, he didn't hear a word that she had said. Sensing that he was probably thinking too hard, she sat down the duffle bag that contained his clothing and other miscellaneous items like, pain medications, body wash for men and underwear. Kicking her high heels off her freshly painted toes, she climbed into the bed with him and snuggled underneath him.

"Tell me what's wrong, handsome," she said as she let her thumb brush against his bruised knuckles.

Yakhi was still thinking about Cyber, not paying her any attention, when they heard voices just outside of his door.

"Yes, girl, he woke up yesterday, after you left. I tried calling you, but I kept getting your voicemail."

"Shit! Has he said anything, has he been bathed yet?"

"No, ma'am. We heard you loud and clear, when you said you didn't want anyone showering your husband. I mean, to be completely honest, I don't blame you. These RN's and CENA's are so damn disrespectful, it's ridiculous."

The nurse said shaking her head at the thought of how thirsty some of the women on her floor was.

"Yeah, I know, that's why I said what I said. I don't mind beating a bitch's ass behind that one in room 315. I'm so pissed that I turned my fucking phone off. I wanted to be here when he woke up, but I had to check on the baby and I just passed out after the appointment."

"Aww, congratulations. Well, come on. Let's get in here and wake him up, I'll help you get him into the bathroom and get him situated," Nurse Lamborghini said, as she opened the door to Yakhi's room.

Walking in the room ahead of Cyber, she was shocked to see that Yakhi was up and had company. She turned on her heels to try and distract Cyber, but it was too late. She was already inside the room and had seen the little tramp lying in bed next to her man. Cyber inhaled calmly and tried to steady her breathing before she spoke.

"I'm trying not to loose my cool up in here, but you got five seconds to get your ass out of my husband's hospital bed and leave right away, before I forget that I'm carrying precious cargo with me and commence to beating the brakes off ya ass." She said, opening her eyes.

"Aye, don't bring that bullshit into my space. What the fuck you even doing up here?" Yakhi spoke up before Aoki could open her mouth.

Confusion spread across her face, as her eyebrows slowly came together, creating a deep, wrinkled unibrow in the center of her forehead.

"Excuse me?"

"You fucking deaf? I said what the fuck are you doing here?"

"First off, you need to check that little bitch ass attitude. Why the fuck do you think I'm here? To check on yo' stubborn ass."

"Man, get-the-fuck-outta-here! My woman said ya ass ain't been up here for the past four days. Fuck you lying for, sweetheart?"

Not only did nurse Lamborghini's face express a state of confusion, so did Cyber's. As if she knew her lies were about to be exposed, Aoki climbed out of the bed and slipped her feet into her high heels. She grabbed her purse from the night stand and started for the door, when he stopped her.

"Baby, hol' up, you ain't gotta go no fucking where. She getting the fuck up outta here," Yakhi said, as he strugged to sit up in the middle of the bed.

Cyber stood there with her hurt emotions on the cusp of her sleeves. Not only was their baby making her emotional, but she was hurt that he would believe anything that his little whore said.

"Umm, I don't mean to butt into you all's conversation, but Mr. Rodriquez, your wife ha—,"

"Well if you didn't mean to butt in, why did you?" He asked with an ice-cold glare taking over his once relaxed expression.

"Anyways, like I was saying, your wife has been here

everyday and night, since you've been admitted into the hospital. I do believe it was her that brought you in covered from head to toe in your blood. I also recall, you being put on the 'do not visit list'," she said, narrowing her gaze in Aoki's direction.

With a perplexed expression on his face, his head turned in Aoki's direction. He then turned and watched as the wet tears painted Cyber's chunky cheeks.

"Shorty, what the fuck they talkin' about?" He turned back in Aoki's direction. Just looking at how she was all the sudden so standoffish let him know that she played him.

Cyber shook her head and headed for the door.

"Mrs. Rodriquez, I am so sorry about all of this, and I will personally see to it that she will be escorted off the premises immediately."

"It's Jackson—Ms. Jackson." She stood a few inches away from the door, as she twisted her wedding ring off her finger and tossed it across the room. Watching as it landed on top of the bedside table, she looked over her shoulder and left with a few parting words.

"You want him so bad, you can have him!"

She walked out of the door, as the sound of Yakhi calling her name filled her ears.

"Man, get the fuck up outta here, bruh!" He barked at Aoki.

When he was alone, he picked the large diamond ring up and stared at it between his fingers. The only thing that ran through his mind was that he'd jumped the gun prematurely . He reached over the bedside table and picked up his cellphone. Browsing through his contacts, he located the number he was looking for. When he did, he sent a decoded text then put his phone down. He laid his head back on the pillow and closed his eyes. So many things were running through his mind, but what stuck out to him was the saying, *"When a good girl turns bad, she's gone forever!"*

21

CYBER

Wanna See A Nigga Squirm, Fuck With His Most Prized Possession

"Ma'am would you like to read over the disclosure form?"

"No, I mean, I think I have the gist of the procedure. You scrape the baby out and in so many words, there could be complications. And if there are any, you won't be held liable. Does that sum up the terms and conditions?"

The nurse stood there flabbergasted at how vulgar her response was. But hey, that's basically what it said, but they used big educated terms to juke you into thinking they really cared about your well-being and safety.

"Umm, okay. I just have a couple of questions for you, then I'll take your questionnaire out to the doctor and he'll be right in to speak with you."

Cyber simply nodded her head, giving the woman the right to proceed.

"Okay good. First question can you verify your name, birthday, address, and insurance information, please?"

"Cyber Hermés Jackson, April 23, 1995, my address is 16500 Quarry road, apt 573 Columbia, South Carolina, 29229. And my insurance carrier is Cigna Insurance."

"Okay, got it. Now who do you live with?"

"I live alone."

"I know you said you live alone, but I still have to ask the question. Do you feel safe at home, or out in the public?"

"Yup! I wish a bitch would run the fuck up on me, I'll slice their ass like a loaf of pound cake," she said, flashing the small razor blade that she had concealed on the inside of her right cheek.

"Ohhkayy, I'll take this out to the doctor, and he'll be in shortly."

Cyber giggled as she watched the nurse scurry out of the exam room. She wasn't a ghetto bird, but the lady was so stuffy and bourgeois that she couldn't resist the opportunity to ruffle her feathers a bit.

Not too long afterward, the doctor came in to talk to her and explained the risk of performing an abortion so late into a pregnancy. He tried several times to get her to try some different alternatives, but Cyber was dead set on terminating the lifeline that would've bonded her and Yakhi together forever. She felt like there was no point of carrying the baby to term, just to give it to someone else. It was a tough decision, but she had to make the best decision for her. She was tired of putting everyone in first place. For once, she wanted to be selfish and think about her wants and needs.

THREE WEEKS HAD PASSED and for the first time in a long time, Cyber felt like she had some clarity about her life. She had returned to SC and found a job working in the art gallery that was just below her apartment. She had even taken a step out on faith and went out with the owner of the gallery, Armez, who had been trying unsuccessfully to take her out on a date since she first moved there. Cyber decided to take him up on his offer. Before, she was conflicted because she was married to Yakhi. As soon as she returned to South Carolina, she hired a lawyer and filed for divorce. So many factors led to her making that move. Her being guilty about not giving Layah up was the biggest one. Him taking Aoki's side without even hearing her out, was the final straw.

The process of going about the divorce was the easy part; getting Yakhi on-board was another task. He was giving her the run around, ducking and dodging the Process Server. After she'd left the hospital, he was blowing her phone down with calls and text messages, but as soon as he got wind of her trying to divorce him, courtesy of her lawyer's voicemails and e-mails, he shut down all forms of communication with her.

He was even smart enough to move from his house out in Farmington Hills. Looking for him was like trying to find Waldo on the poster at the River Rouge Library, as a kid. She eventually put her divorce on hold, but that didn't mean her life was going to stop. Cyber had so many new changes in her life that she had to adjust to; too many to be running the streets trying to get her husband to end their union.

With that mindset, she decided to give Armez a shot. Their night started off perfect. He sent her on a scavenger hunt, with clues about where they were going and what to wear. From his clues, it was obvious that she had to wear something conservative, and with her current situation, she didn't even want to look at her body, much less find something form fitting to wear. But she pulled the task off, settling for something elegant, but loose fitting.

Armez blind-folded her and took her to Illinois. He reserved a yacht for just the two of them from SunSea Yacht Charters company, where they sailed on the quiet waters of Lake Michigan. The whole ambiance was something out of a romance movie. From the hanging chandelier lights, to the live jazz band on-board, all the way down to the chef catered, five-course meal, Cyber couldn't stop smiling the entire night.

After the boat tour was over, they got a room overlooking the Chicago skyline. The whole night, they sat on the terrace enjoying the mild breeze, talking about where they saw their lives headed in the next five years. It was refreshing to get to know someone who wasn't physically involved in the streets and didn't curse after every sentence.

Cyber was shocked that she was there in that moment. If someone would've told her a year ago, that she would've met a man who changed her perception on the male species, she would've probably tried to strike them. She never thought that she would open up and click with not one guy, but two. As she laid down that night, she thanked the Lord for showing her something different.

Her hand caressed her hardened abdomen as she drifted into dreamland.

22

YAKHIYAH

WAVING THE WHITE FLAG

"Hi, I have a delivery for a Ms. Yakhiyah Rodriquez," the delivery man said, holding onto a huge vase concealed by plastic, shielding the three dozen pink roses inside.

Peachy, her administrative assistant, signed for the flowers and then walked them to her boss's office. Tapping on the wooden frame three time, she was rewarded with Yakhiyah's alluring big, brown eyes.

"Delivery."

"Delivery, for who?"

"For you!" She said blushing, like someone had sent the flowers to her.

"Are you being serious right now?" Yakhiyah inquired, as she stood to her feet, smoothing out the tiny wrinkles in her beige pencil skirt. She walked over toward the door and reached for the vase.

"Dead serious, boss lady. The guy just dropped them

off," she said as she watched Hiyah carry the flowers to her desk, removing the plastic on the way there.

She picked up the card and read the inscription that was in bold block letters.

"The battle ain't over until the trophy has been obtained!"

A smirk covered her face, followed by her rolling her eyes.

"You're the trophy, shawty," his deep voice resonated through the large space around them.

"How did you get back here?" She said over her shoulder.

"You don't know the kind of nigga you fuckin' wit'?"

"Oh, trust me, I know the kind of nigga you are," she said, turning around to face him.

"Aye, I didn't come here to beef wit' chu, I just came to take you out."

"You askin' me out, or telling me you taking me out?"

He smiled a gorgeous smile, as he stroked his chest length beard.

"I'm asking you out on a date," he said, pulling a small, stuffed red and brown humming bird out of his pants pocket, that was attached to a long rectangular box.

"Saa, what is that?"

"Come see," he said, extending the presents out in her direction.

She stood with her back facing the desk, chewing on her bottom lip, contemplating her next move. She wasn't trying to go there with Saafiq again. She was really inter-ested in seeing where her friendship with Luka could go.

"Ya-Ya," he whispered to her soul.

Determined not to give in so easily, she stood there for a few more seconds and then she walked over toward him. She took the gifts out of his hand, opening the velvet box. Her eyes bounced around all the baguette diamonds that covered the entire bracelet. It was the most gorgeous gift she had ever received. Sure, she was used to her twin brother, Yakhi, buying her gifts all the time, but this gift meant something else.

When she was in a relationship with her ex, O'Saum, he never brought her gifts like that. His idea of being romantic was getting a couple flowers from the local Kroger's grocery store. It meant more to her that he had surprised her with flowers and came bearing gifts, it showed her that he was taking the initative to try and mend fences. That had scored him a few brownie points. So, the least she could do was hear him out over dinner that he was going to pay for.

YAKHIYAH AND SAAFIQ sat at a table in the back of Irides-cence in Motor City casino. For the first five minutes, he just sat there and watched her every move. She felt shy under his intense glare.

"Why you looking like that, boo boo?"

"Why you staring at me like that?" She asked, swirling the red wine around in her glass.

"What, I can't stare at you now?" He asked with his hands extended in front of him.

"It's just weird, real borderline creep-ish." She took a sip of her Merlot and then set her glass back on the table.

"I'm just admiring your beauty that's all."

Yakhiyah just nodded her head, as her eyes looked around the beautiful, upscale restaurant. Her eyes were intrigued with the light purple décor around her. The silk, sliver linen's and shiny silverware was a huge step up from the plastic forks and knives from fast food joints, that's what she was used to. Growing up with a dope boy for a brother, you become accustomed to fast food and some nice food establishments, but those days were few and far in between.

Yakhi didn't want to expose his sister to his gutter lifestyle, so he kept her sheltered from it. He taught her not to get too caught up with the extravagant things his lifestyle could afford her. He always wanted her to remain humble and remember where she came from. So, when someone like Saafiq brought her to a five-star restaurant like Iridescence, she would appreciate it.

"But you know what?"

"What?" She asked, not making eye contact.

Reaching across the table, he grabbed her hands and interlocked hers with his. Her head turned and she looked at him, giving him her undivided attention.

"I want to apologize for not being the nigga that you needed."

Yakhiyah's eyes dropped down at the speck of wine running down the stem of the champagne flute.

"Naw, look at me. I'm dead fucking serious right now, shawty."

Doing as she was told, she looked up into his cognac colored eyes.

"I'm sorry for playing with your feelings. I'm sorry for not being man enough for you. A nigga was dead ass out here moving like a fuck nigga, snorting zans, fucking different kinda bitches, just all kinds of shit that would have you out here looking stupid as fuck. I been thinking about you—about us. I wanna make shit right between us."

"Saafiq, I—,"

"Wait, let me finish. I'm sitting here asking you for forgiveness. I want you to forgive me for all the nights I made you cry. Forgive me for all the uncomfortable nights you had without me. Forgive me for being out and about with these hoes. Forgive me for giving ya dick away, and for spitting game in these hoes ear, when I should've been in yours telling you how beautiful you are. How worthy you are, how you deserve the moon and the stars. And how you deserve to be somebody's wife," he said, pulling out a white, square box.

By that point, she had started to cry, but she began to hyperventilate when she saw him pulling out the ring box.

"Saafiq, don't play right now. Wh—what is that?" She asked, as she pointed at the box in his hands.

"I would never play with your emotions like that. Will you allow me the opportunity to make shit right between us. I wanna be your husband. Can I be that?"

"Saafiq, I can't believe you—," Before she could finish her sentence, they heard loud clapping coming from a few tables over.

"Damn, that was an exceptional proposal. Not quite like the one I had prepared to say, but it was pretty decent, never the less." Turning to look over at Yakhiyah, he tossed a black box on the table toward her.

"I guess I don't have to get down on one knee or nothing, so I'ma just ask you to forgive me, and let's move forward. You don't have to worry about Angela and my son, OJ, because I have that situation handled already. Yakhiyah Rodriquez, will you marry me?" He stood there casually with both of his hands stuffed inside his pockets, waiting on an answer.

Yakhiyah hadn't paid O'Saum any more attention after she saw him coming her way a few seconds before his bullshit ass speech. With her eyes on Saafiq, she sat back some in her seat and swallowed the rest of her drink.

"How do you know that you want to spend the rest of your life with me? You do know that a marriage is forever, right?"

His eyebrows crinkled, and he sat up in his seat.

"Why you tryna play me, shawty?"

"I'm not trying to play you, I'm simply asking you a question," she said, setting the glass on the table.

"Naw, yes you are. It's cool, aye but look, ask yourself this, can you see yourself spending the rest of your life with me?" He asked, sitting up in his chair.

"Yes, with no hesitation. Now answer my question." She said, eye contact never wavering.

He just sat there and stared at her.

"Umm, I believe I asked you a gotdamn question. Maybe I didn't make myself clear earlier. This proposal isn't optional. There really is only one answer that's accept—,"

"No! Actually, it's hell fucking no!" She said, turning to look in his direction.

"Saafiq, give me my ring and let's go," she said, holding her ring finger out toward him.

"Yakhiyah, don't let that nigga put that fucking ring on ya finger," he sneered snatching both boxes off the table.

Saafiq stood to his feet calmly and sucker punched O'Saum in the jaw, sending the ring boxes flying between his legs.

"I didn't interrupt ya faggot ass, as you stood there copping pleas. I minded my business and let *my* woman speak for herself, but what the fuck I won't tolerate is the fucking disrespect. When you see a queen amongst your presence, you bow the fuck down and show her some got damn respect. Now she told ya ass hell naw, so move the fuck around nigga!" He barked.

O'Saum sat up on the floor, watching as Saafiq slid the ring onto her finger and kissed his woman on her lips. Just as they were getting ready to walk away, he pulled out his gun and cocked it back. Because Fiq wasn't paying him any attention, he didn't see Yakhiyah, jump on top of him, securing her legs around his waist, covering his torso as O'Saum fired four shots into her body.

"Babb—baby I—I love you," she whispered, as her body fell limp in his arms.

23

SAAFIQ

In A Split Second, Your Whole World could Crumble

He sat with his head back, eyes closed tightly, trying to fight back the tears that wouldn't leave him alone. All the noise around him had been drowned out by his thoughts. Images of her beautiful face sitting upright across from him in the restaurant wouldn't let him be. Tired of being uncomfortable, his eyes opened and looked down at all the blood that covered his hands and the tan dress shirt he had on. That was all it took, for the small tears to come racing down his cheeks.

He hopped up out of his seat and rushed over to the receptionist desk, to get an update on Yakhiyah's condition.

"Aye, ma'am, can you give me an update on Yakhiyah Rodriquez?" He pled, just as Yakhi and Mr. and Mrs. Rodriquez came rushing into the emergency department.

"Yo' Fiq, what the fuck happened, bruh?" Yakhi yelled, seemingly out of breath.

Saafiq turned around and couldn't help the tears that raced down his face, as he watched the man, he called his brother in agonizing pain, holding his chest as if he was having a heart attack.

"Bruhh, I was going to come to you and talk to you man to man. I've been dealing with Ya-Ya for the past year, way before we started working together. We were kicking it for a hot little minute and then I fell back, because shit started getting deeper than I was willing to deal wit' at the time. Tonight, I decided I didn't wanna spend the rest of my life not knowing how it felt to have a normal heartbeat. Bruh, ya fucking sister is my muthafuckin' rib, bruh. On some serious shit, I love the fuck outta that girl G." He rambled on.

"Nigga, what the fuck happened?" He yelled as he paced back and forth.

"I took her to dinner and proposed, and then her bitch ass ex came at shawty sideways wit' his whack ass proposal. I beat his ass for disrespecting her and then the pussy tried to shoot me, but ended up shooting her."

"What the fuck you mean he ended up shooting her?" he spoke through gritted teeth.

Saafiq took a deep breath, as his hands covered the front of his face. He knew some shit was about to pop once he told him what his sister did.

"She jumped on me and he shot her in the back."

Without warning, Yakhi hauled off and punched Saafiq in the face. He wasn't going to fight him back. If he had been told some shit like that, he would've hit his mans too, but Yakhi took it a step further, when he snuck him while he was already on the ground. The two men went at it like two strangers in the street, until the security guards and Mr. Rodriquez tried to break them up.

"I want these two out of here!" Yelled the receptionist, as she tried to pick the table of magazines up that they flipped over.

"You two need to go, before they call the police," Racquel Rodriquez said.

"Man, fuck that shit. That's my fucking wife up in there shot the fuck up. Y'all can call God for all the fuck I care, I ain't leaving until I see my wife." Saa said, spitting blood from his busted lip, on the floor.

"Fuck outta here, nigga, she ain't shit to yo' ass. How the fuck you supposed to be my mans, but can't even keep it real with ya nigga and tell me you fuckin' on my little sister nigga?"

"Man, Khi, look. I ain't the nigga to beef wit', I shoot to kill. I swear to God by the time I knew y'all was related, I had already started falling for shawty, on my ole girl."

"When the fuck did you find out?" He gritted.

"The day we stopped by her crib, and shawty was flipping on ya about ya ditching her because she thought ya had a bitch in the whip."

Yakhi stood in the middle of the floor, eye red and

swelling by the second, with his hands on the top of his head, as he thought back to the day Saafiq was talking about.

"Sir, we've called the police. We can't have you guys up in here tearing up our waiting room and disturbing the peace." The lady said walking back to the check-in desk.

"Listen, you two need to get a fucking grip and make the fuck up. You two get out of here and come back tomorrow with a clearer head. Now kiss and make up!" Racquel said.

"Man, fuck outta here! Fuck that nigga, man!" Yakhi said.

Whap. Whap.

His mother popped him upside his head twice and then shoved him toward the door.

"I said get your butt on outta here Yakhi Neoqi, I won't say it again. You too, Saafiq."

Both men looked at each other and then walked out to their vehicles.

Saafiq sat up in the uncomfortable seat. Wiping his eyes, he realized he was still sitting in his car, parked in the hospital parking lot. He looked at the clock on his dashboard and realized he had been sleeping in the car for two hours. There was no way that he was leaving that hospital until he saw his wife.

He wiped his hands over his face, just as he watched the rude ass receptionist walking out, carrying her lunch pail and a roll-a-way book bag. He was so happy that he couldn't contain himself. He hopped out the car and ran into the hospital. Because someone new was on shift, the man seated behind the desk wasn't privy to the situation that happened between him and Yakhi. He got her room number and ran toward the elevators.

As soon the doors opened, he walked on, stood toward the back of the elevator and laid his head on the wall. Watching the numbers increase the higher up he went, his mind soared. It wasn't until he walked off the elevator that the thought of seeing her laid up in a hospital bed with a million and one tubes running through her skin, in her mouth and her nose. Even feeling that way, he still had to see her. There was no way he was going to just leave her high and dry.

He walked slowly down the hallway, until he found her room number. His feet stilled, his heart raced, and he started to sweat out of nowhere. Saafiq was trying to calm his nerves so he wouldn't have a panic attack. He started to turn around and walk back down the hallway but was stopped by someone coming out her room. He looked down at her mother and gave her a small smile.

"C'mon son, there's nothing to be afraid of," Yakhiyah's mother said, as she grabbed his arm and led him in the room.

Saafiq had to bite his bottom lip to keep from

screaming out. She looked so peaceful lying there. Her mother must've braided her hair back into one long braid, because earlier in the night, her hair was down and freshly flat ironed. He slowly walked over to the bed, leaned over and kissed her on the forehead then softly on the lips. Standing back upright, he looked down at her still facial features. If he wasn't there to witness what happened, he would've thought that she was just sleeping.

"What's on your mind, son?" He turned and looked at her mother sitting down in the rocker near the window, as she knitted what looked like a hat.

"Just thinking about how she took those bullets for me. Like, she really jumped on me and took four bullets for me," He said, feeling the arrival of his tears.

"Yes, my little baby has always been quite the protector. She ran around my house acting like she was Yakhi's mother. Whenever he got into trouble, she was right there like his public defender. I couldn't stand it then, but then I came to realize, that was just who Yakhiyah was. She's feisty and, has a loud, combustible mouthpiece, but she always means well," her mother said, focusing on the stitch she'd just created.

"I know, but as a man, I just can't—,"

"You will. Do not make this about your pride. Just because she took a few bullets for you, it doesn't tarnish your role in your relationship. She would never look down her nose at you because of a decision she decided to make."

Saafiq stood there nodding his head, giving her a silent understanding. "I just keep thinking about the whole situation with Ya—,"

"Don't! He'll come around. Allow him to process this tragedy by himself. When he's ready to talk to you, he will. And don't worry about not telling him about you and my daughter. He'll get over that too."

"Thanks, Mrs. Rodriquez, I really appreciate the pep talk."

"Call me ma or Racquel. And you're most certainly welcome."

"Okay, Mrs. Racquel. Is it okay if I ask for Yakhiyah's hand in marriage? I know it's a bit late for that, but I would really appreciate it if you would say—,"

"Yes!"

Saafiq chuckled. In ways, Racquel reminded him of his mother. Both women were head strong with a tongue so vicious, it could cut a Rattlesnake's head completely off!

"You don't let anyone get a word in edge-wise, do you?"

"No need to, especially when I already know what it is, you're going to say."

"How, when I haven't even finished my sentence?"

"A mother just knows."

"I can respect that."

"Baby, you had no choice in the matter. Mama gone get up out of here and give you two some privacy. If she happens to—,"

"Wake up, you'll be the first person I call," he said, looking over at her with a smirk on his face.

Racquel stood to her feet and punched him in the arm. She grabbed her bag of yarn and all her belongings and quietly left the room.

"Baby, I'm so sorry. I should've protected you. Fuck, I just keep fucking up man!" He barked.

Saafiq walked closer to the bed and held her hand. His thumb brushing gently over her knuckles.

"Fuck you doing in here, nigga?"

Saafiq blew out a harsh breath and closed his eyes, praying to God to help him control his temper. There was only so much of his smart remarks that he was going to take. He didn't want to take it there with him, because he didn't want to beef wit his brother. That and he knew how Yakhiyah felt about her twin brother, but as a man he wasn't built to just let a nigga bully him. Shit wasn't rockin' like that, brother or not!

"I'm just trying to see my wife, bruh."

"Nigga, fuck you. I ain't give ya pussy ass my permission to marry my sister, nigga!" He yelled.

"Look here, bruh, I love ya ass like the brother I never had! Although I fucked up, you still gon' respect me as a muthafuckin' man, my G!" Saafiq barked, hitting himself in the chest.

"Nigga, all that shit got cancelled out the moment you lied about fucking on my little sister!" He yelled, stepping closer to Saafiq.

"You think if I would've known earlier that she was your sister, I would've still pursued her? Hell naw, I wouldn't have, the shit just happened. By the time I knew y'all were related, the shit was too fucking late!"

"Man, get the fuck outta here with that bullshit. When you first found the fuck out, you should've told me. I don't want my fucking sister dealing with a nigga like you!"

"Word, and what kinda nigga am I?"

"The type of nigga that's money driven. The type of nigga that don't respect a real woman, categorizing her with these other hoes in the streets. You the type of nigga I wouldn't want my cat dating, nigga, fucking is you talking about? My muthafuckin' sister is my heart, nigga. I'll die behind her ass, can you say the same?"

"Hell, yeah, I can! I ain't never felt this way about no bitch I done smashed in the past. This shit is deeper than just some pussy. Remember a while back when I was fucked up behind some chick, ya sister was the chick. Nigga, yeah, I've—,"

"Dead it, nigga! The shit ain't gon' work. You ain't about to have my sister looking and acting like these dumb ass birds in the D, all because you can't keep ya piece in ya jeans nigga."

"Will y'all shut the fuck up? I'm trying to sleep here," the sound of her hoarse voice cut in.

Saafiq turned around so fast, he damn near tripped over his own two feet.

"Baby, you up?" He asked, running over to her bedside.

"I didn't plan on being up, but yeah, I'm up," she said, trying to scoot herself up in the bed, but she couldn't move her weakened body.

"Ya-Ya, don't try to move and shit, let me go get the doctor," Saafiq said, as he laid her back down and then rushed out the room looking for a doctor.

"You know you were dead ass wrong for talking to him like that."

"Man, whatever, let's talk about that dumb ass stunt you pulled!"

"It wasn't a stunt, I was protecting my husband. Same way I look after you and papa."

"He a grown ass man, he don't need that kind of protecting. And if he does, he ain't the nigga for you."

"He most certainly is the nigga for me. Khi, I'm grown, I don't need you interfering in my love life. I know what's best for me and he is it! I love you, but you can't hold onto my hand forever. How do you expect me to grow, if I never make any mistakes, or if I always let you come save the day, Superman?"

"There is nothing you can say to try to convince me to be okay with this. My best fucking friend, Neoqia?"

"Well too damn bad, Neoqi. I love him, I'm going to marry him, and you and papa are going to walk me down the aisle with a smile on your faces," she said, opening her eyes.

Yakhi started to say something, but the doctor, two nurses and Saafiq rushed into the room.

As the doctor did his assessment, Yakhiyah kept her eyes glued on Saafiq. She felt bad seeing the fear isolated in his retinas. She continued to look at him even while she answered all the doctor's questions. It was her way of assuring him that she was okay. Her eyes may have been on his, but, out of her peripheral, she could see the petite nurse with the red and blonde 20-inch weave eying her man. She had to put an end to whatever fantasy she had brewing in her mind. Shot the fuck up or even dead, she would come back reincarnated just to fuck a bitch up behind Saafiq Harlen Daniels.

"Umm, baybeeeee girllll, you must have an eye problem or something, not sure, and I really don't care. But umm, if you don't want corrective surgery on ya bug eyes, I would suggest that you keep them focused on what Dr. Gamble is talking about, because he's taken, oh—and so is he," she said in an animated voice resembling Instagram comedian B. Simone.

TWO WEEKS HAD PASSED and Yakhiyah was still in the hospital. It was a miracle according to doctor's Gamble and O'hygi. If she had turned her body slightly to the left when she hopped up on Saafiq, one of the four, or possibly all four bullets, would've ended her life. They were keeping her at Providence hospital for a few more weeks. They wanted to monitor the scar tissue that was near her spine and help her with physical therapy, since she hadn't been out of the bed since the accident.

Saafiq was at Twelve-Oaks mall getting Yakhiyah some much needed clothes and feminine hygiene products, when he saw a familiar face in the crowd. Abandoning the things in his hand, he ran out of Bath and Body Works, and took off down the long walkway. He didn't care that he was bumping into people. The only thing on his mind at the moment was his target. It seemed as if the person was walking on air as he glided further and further into the deep crowd. Panic started to set in the more people crowded his line of sight.

It had gotten so bad, all he could see was a small patch on the person's coat. Feeling like he was left with no choice, he pulled his Taurus 608 .357 Magnum revolver with the dark stained wooden handle from the small of his back, upped his weapon and fired four shots into O'Saum's back.

Once the sound of gunshots erupted into the air, people started running in every direction, providing a quick cover for him, as he too rushed toward the fire exit. He slipped right through the door undetected. The loud siren on the door blared piercingly, but he continued to high tail it across the parking lot. As soon as he made it safely inside his truck, he heard police sirens. That was his cue to get the fuck on down. He wasn't trying to go to prison for a murder wrap, but if he had to, he would. Her love and loyalty warranted that.

24

SHREECE

I Hate Love

"How did I get here? I don't know the person that's constantly looking back at me in the dusty window. How did I go from being the head nurse in the NICU at Detroit Children's hospital, number one in my class in high school and at Wayne State University, had my own car, job and house, the epitome of independent, to sharing a cell and a bunk bed with some woman I didn't know, having to be told when I could wake up and go to bed, only being allowed out in general population for one hour out of twenty-four damn hours?

How did I get here? I guess the better question was why did I let love ruin my life? I had gotten so consumed with trying to improve my relationship before he lost interest in what we had, that I stopped loving myself. I let love reduce me to the insecure, dependent murderer I was today. This wasn't how my life was supposed to go."

Shreece thought, as she sat inside the court room awaiting on the jury to decide her fate. Shreece had been charged with one count of premeditated murder, reckless endangerment to a minor, vehicular homicide and one count of criminally negligent manslaughter because she was the cause of Izzoni's suicide.

She wasn't convinced that her legal counsel had pursued the jury. If she was one of the jurors, she would've found herself guilty. Her team consisted of a bunch of rookies; freshly bar passed attorney's. They played hard ball, but they weren't as polished as she imagined in her mind, and no-where near as seasoned as the state's prosecutors.

The door that lead to a small room that housed a large rectangular table with plush chairs that easily accommodated twelve of her peers, opened and in a single file line, they walked out of the room and began to take their seats. A short, snobby, white man who was in dire need of a haircut, stood within the box they were seated in, shoulders back, glasses sitting on the tip of his nose, as he held a tiny piece of paper in his hands.

"All rise! The honorable Judge Ameada Laurent presiding. You may take your seats."

Shreece watched as the short, thick black lady took a seat in her oversized office chair. Her eyes seemed to have found Shreece's quickly. She shrank down in her seat as she watched the judge rolling her eyes. Ever since she was assigned her trial date, the name of the judge haunted her. She couldn't for the life of herself recall where she had heard that name before.

Sitting there looking at the lady intently, it finally dawned on her. She was one of the thirsty thot bitches thirsting it up in Izzoni's DM's. She cussed her ass out so bad that Ameada ended up blocking her and Izzoni on IG. She knew then that she had fucked up to the highest power.

"I'm guessing you all have reached a conclusion in Ms. Montgomery's case?"

"Yes, your honor, we have," the Balding man said.

"All rise," she said dryly.

Everyone stood to their feet, as the balding guy got ready to read her fate, from the tiny piece of paper.

"On count one, premeditated murder in the case of Sionei Miller, what say you?"

"For count one, we the jury, find the defendant *guilty* of premeditated murder."

"On count two, reckless endangerment to a minor and vehicular homicide for Alana Jordan, what say you?"

"On count two, we the jury find the defendant *guilty*."

"And finally, to the third count of criminally negligent manslaughter of Izzoni savage, what say you?"

"We find the defendant *guilty* of the charge for count three."

"Ms. Montgomery, I usually schedule another hearing

date for sentencing, but because I can't stand to see your face one more day, I am going to sentence you right now. You are the worst kind of murderer I've ever seen in the five years that I have been serving as a civil servant. Unfortunately, here in Michigan, we do not carry the death penalty. If we did, I would sentence you to death. You deserve to die for what you did. There is no justice in jail time for you because jail time is a slap in the justice system's face!" The judge spat. She paused to look over a bunch of papers that were in front of her.

Shreece stood there with tears in her eyes, as she physically held onto the table for support. She just knew that at any moment, her knees were going to give out on her.

"Okay, so because you have three different offenses, that range differently in terms of a sentence, I'm going to give you the minimum sentence allowed. I hear by sentence you to 22 years in prison. You will be placed in the custody of the Michigan Department of Corrections. You will be transferred to Huron Valley Correctional Facility for women, where you will serve out your sentence. Do you wish to make a statement?"

Still standing there in a state of shock, the whole courtroom quieted down to see if she would make a statement or plead for a lesser sentence. She did neither of the sort. Shreece stood there staring blankly into space. Court had wrapped up, her attorneys were standing around talking to one another and she stood still, staring at her past, until the deputies came and carted her off to her cell.

SHREECE REMAINED in the county jail, until they were able to set up her intake process. Generally, an inmate would stay in the county jail from anywhere between ten to thirty days, until they were ready to move them off to the prison facility.

Shreece laid on her cold cement cot and stared at the ceiling, thinking. There was no way that she would last 22 years in prison. It was crazy how she wasn't remorseful for killing Sionei. She was genuinely hurt and confused as to why Izzoni would flip on her like that. After all the good times they shared, he was just as fraud as the next nigga running the streets in Detroit.

She felt like she had eliminated the problem for the two of them. Unbeknownst to her, she was the problem for him. Turning over on her side, she stared down at the silver nail file she had confiscated from her bunky. She had been playing with it; sharpening its pointy edge, since she came back from court. Her thoughts ran wild, as the thought of being able to confront and be with Izzoni crossed her mind. All she had to do was slit the right vein and she and he could be reunited.

"Yeah, that could work," she whispered, running her fingertips along the biggest vein on her wrist.

Hearing footsteps, she slid the weapon down further into the tiny slit she had made on the side of the thin mattress. She closed her eyes and pretended to be asleep.

Her thoughts traveled to heaven, then hell and back, as she decided to hold off on her plan until the morning time.

"You ain't getting rid of me that easily, Izzy," she mumbled to herself.

25

YAKHIYAH

Fighting Myself, For us

It had been a few days and Yakhiyah just wasn't feeling her life at that moment. She had been totally dependent on Saafiq to basically do everything for her, from wiping her butt and her vagina, to showering her and sometimes feeding her. She wasn't used to depending on anyone besides her brother. Not being able to wipe your own ass was depressing in itself. She hadn't regained the strength in her legs, and she flat out refused to go to physical therapy. Her bitchy behavior was putting a strain on her and Saafiq's relationship. Every time he went to do something for her, she would cop an attitude and start an argument, because she didn't know how to deal with not being able to get up and go on her own.

The fighting between the two of them had gotten so bad that Saafiq started sleeping in her guest bedroom. It was late at night and Saafiq had just stormed out of the house because she wanted to argue about him not wanting her trying to get up and cook him dinner. Yakhiyah was over the moon that he wanted to marry her, when it initially happened, but after the shooting, she wasn't even sure that she wanted to get married anymore.

With how she was raised, and how she felt as a woman preparing herself for marriage, she should've been doing all his cooking and laundry, but she couldn't because she didn't have the strength in her lower limbs or her arms. Lying up in a hospital bed for four weeks made her recovery twice as hard. Her body had basically deteriorated. She even accumulated a couple bed sores on her back and buttocks.

Yakhiyah was thoroughly disgusted with herself and her life. It frustrated her that Fiq had been nothing but supportive. He never once complained about having to clean her up or after her. He took it all in stride, telling her on more than one occasion that he was forever indebted to her. The roles could've easily been reversed. He was just grateful that he had someone who cared enough about him to risk their life to save his. But what he couldn't take was the daily pity parties she wanted to have. He wanted her to embrace the fact that Jesus had spared her life. He wanted her to be grateful that she had a man like him in her corner. Saafiq told her on numerous occasions that she wasn't a burden on him. But that always seemed to go in one ear and out the other.

Yakhiyah laid in the bed looking through her photos. She had taken a few off-guard shots of him when he had come to visit her in the hospital. Tears trickled down her cheeks, as she thought about losing the only man that had the ability to set her soul on fire. Being around Saafiq day in and day out, helped her learn more about herself as a grown woman. Her tumlutrous relationship with O'Saum taught her all the things she didn't like about herself as a young girl blooming into a woman. There were things she had tolerated with O'Saum that were simply off limits in her new relationship, and in any relationship after Saafiq, if the two of them didn't work out.

Saafiq showed her how to value herself, how not to settle for what someone else felt she deserved. She felt bad for the way she had treated him. Deciding to be a woman and apologize, she called him.

Ring. Ring.

"Hello," the sing-song voice answered.

Yakhiyah took the phone off her ear and looked at her screen.

"Helloooo," the voice said, again.

"Who is this?" Yakhiyah said calmly.

"You called this number, so who is this?"

She blew out a deep breath and counted to ten in her head. She was trying not to pre-judge him based off her ex's past. So, she cleared her throat and tried an easy-going approach.

"I called looking for my husband. Is he around by any

chance?" She bit the inside of her bottom lip, trying to coax herself to calm down and not jump up and go find his ass, cutting his dick off in the process for allowing a bitch to be ballsy enough to answer his cell phone.

The better question to ask was why his phone was out of his pocket, just lying around for someone to pick up and browse through or answer his personal calls?

"Ohhh, this must be the beautiful Yakhiyah. Hi, Hiyah, are you feeling better?"

Her eyebrows furrowed and confusion consumed her already heightened temper. She prayed to God that he wasn't pillow talking with some bitch.

"I'm blessed. Again, is Saafiq around?"

"Yeah, hold on."

Yakhiyah listened closely to the background, as the girl went looking for Fiq. She heard him ask the girl why she answered his phone, and she simply replied that it had rang.

"Hello."

Her head fell backward, as she listened to his sexy voice flowing through the receiver.

"Hello."

"Who was that, that answered your phone?" She asked, not wasting any time with the pleasantries.

"My little cousin, Amira. Look, shawty, what's up?" He questioned in a dismissive tone. The way he was talking to her hurt her feelings.

"Where you at?"

"I'm over Mega's crib. She was having a get together," he said dryly.

"Your—your mother invited you over and didn't invite me?" Now she was really in her feelings. Here she was wallowing in her misery and he was out with his family having a good ole time.

"She did invite you. We haven't been talking like that, so I didn't think you would want to come. Seeing as how you don't want me to do shit for you, how was you going to get here?"

Yakhiyah swallowed the thick glob of mucus that was lodged in her throat, as more tears burned her bottom eye lids. She felt like he didn't invite her because he didn't want to be around her. It was true that she wasn't herself as of late, but if the roles were reversed, she would've still invited him.

"Is that the reason, or did you not invite me because you're sick of me?"

"Sick of you? nawl. Sick of your funky ass attitude, hell muthafuckin' yeah! I'm tired of you moping around like ya ass is waiting on death to come take ya ass out. I don't know how much more of that shit I can take bruh," he said, huffing and puffing.

By this time, she allowed the tears to freely express her mood at that moment. She didn't try to hide the sniffing that was a dead giveaway that she was upset. It seemed like all the progress they made in terms of getting to the perfect (as close to perfect) picture of a relationship and then marriage, had been tarnished.

"Well, if that's how you feel, you don't have to deal with me anymore. I can have my brother box up all your shit and send it to your mother's house tonight."

"Fuck you just say?" His voice elevated.

"I said you don't have to deal with me anymore, since I'm such a fucking burden. You think I want to wake up every morning feeling depressed, ugly and not like myself? Well, I don't. I can't even wipe my own fucking ass, Saafiq! So, from this point forward, you don't have to worry about me and my worrisome ass."

"You act like I asked you to take a fucking bullet for me. I didn't ask you to do that shit. I've been doing everything in my fucking power to help you heal and get back to yourself, but ya funky ass is stubborn as fuck. Won't go to physical therapy, won't get the fuck outta the bed, won't let me make love to you or nothing else. So, what the fuck is the point, Yakhiyah?" He yelled so loud, he caught the attention of his mother.

"Don't scream at me like that!" She sobbed.

"Shit, that's the only way to get through to ya mean ass. I can't sweet talk you cuz ya hard headed ass don't hear shit I say, man."

"What the hell is going on in here? Why you hollering like that? I can hear ya ass all the way outside," Mega said, swatting him upside the head.

"I'm sorry, mama, just talking to ya hard headed ass

daughter," He said, getting ready to walk away to finish their conversation in private.

"Give it here. I told ya ass to bring my baby. Hello, Hiy —Hiyah, why you crying?" She asked, as she turned her attention to her son.

"He said, what?"

"I don't give a fuck what he said, y'all ain't breaking up. Yeah, he told me about what's been going on. You need to get out of that funk and let your husband help you out, Hiyah."

Saafiq stood back and listened to the one-sided conversation his mother and his fiancée were having. He was glad someone else was telling her the same shit he had told her a million times before. Most men would get mad, if their woman ignored what they said, only to take heed to the same advice he'd told his woman before from someone else. But as you guessed it, he wasn't like most dudes. He was just happy that his woman was listening to what his mother was saying. He missed the old Yakhiyah, who was always so confident, opinionated, open-minded, loving and affectionate.

Living with her while she was fresh out of the hospital was like living in hell on earth. In his mind, any-one who could sway her to get her mojo back was a damn good way to go. He only said he wanted out to get a reaction out of her. Saafiq was tired of the unfazed Yakhiyah. The woman he'd been cohabitating with wasn't his woman that was usually so upbeat and happy. When he heard her break down on the other end of the line, he knew that he had gotten to her. He truly wanted the best for her, and he knew he had what it took to help bring her greatness out.

"Ma, let me see the phone."

"Okay, sweetie, cut out all that damn crying and fight for a healthy marriage," she said, passing the phone back to her son and then exiting the room.

"You sure her ass ain't pregnant?" Mega asked, as she leaned into him.

"Hell, no I'm not. I heard you Me-Me." Hiyah yelled through the phone.

Mega walked off laughing. She wished they'd hurry up and make her a glam mama.

"When I get home, I want you naked in bed." He said, speaking into the phone.

"No, I'm not fucking with you like that, Saa."

"Ya-Ya, you heard what the fuck I said, right?"

The line had gotten quiet and Yakhiyah started thinking about what her mother in-law had just told her. She didn't want to lose the good thing she had in Saafiq, so she was going to do whatever to get back on the right track.

"Ya-Ya, did you hear—,"

"I heard you, Papi," she whispered into the phone.

"Bet! I want that ass soaking wet, Ya," he whispered seductively into the phone.

"Okay, Papi," she said, pinching her hardened nipples.

"When I get home, I'm going to bathe you and then

fuck you in every position known to man," he said, making his way to his truck.

"Babe, you know I'm not as flexible as I was before the shooting."

"What the fuck I just say? Don't try to tell me how to handle my shit. All that belongs to me. You heard me?"

"Yes Papi,"

Instead of giving up on her or finding some new bitch to wet his dick up, he was going to end his night pampering his future wife.

"Thank you for loving me, flaws and all." She whispered into the phone.

"That's what a real man does. I told you I'm gon' always hold you down. Even if shit don't work out between us, I got chu for life, shawty."

"Don't talk like that, I'm not going anywhere, and neither are you!"

"Facts, boo boo! I'm on my way, beautiful."

"Okay, be safe."

"Already."

"Saafiq?"

"Yes, Mrs. Daniels?"

"I love you."

"I love you more, shawty, on my ole girl," he said, ending the call. He left shortly after and headed home to his beautiful, future wife.

26

CYBER

A Bitch That's Always One Step Ahead Of The Game

Boom. Boom. Boom

The pounding on her front door jolted her from her peaceful slumber. She sat up in the middle of her bed confused. As soon as she sat up, she started rubbing her sore lower back, as she waited to see if the noise she thought she heard was just a figment of her imagination. It was so quiet, she thought maybe she dreamed the whole thing. *That* was until the loud noise started back up. This time, it sounded like her unexpected visitor was now beating on her bedroom window.

Swinging her huge legs over the side of the bed, she stood to her feet, eyes shut tightly as the pain radiated through her back. Ever since her visit to the abortion clinic a couple weeks before, she had been having the strangest pain in her lower back and abdomen. Some would say the pain was normal given the circumstance, but she thought something else was going on. Cyber glanced at herself as she limped passed the mirror she had hanging on her wall. She looked down at the oversized night shirt, and the huge poufy pink bonnet on her head. She said a prayer in her head, hoping that it wasn't a sexy ass guy beating on her door for some kind of assistance.

Shaking her head, Cyber trekked over to the door and opened it. With the door barely open, after she turned the lock, a powerful push from the door sent her flying backward into the potted plant and then onto the floor. She sat up on her butt and looked into his angry, dark, brown eyes.

"Why the fuck is the muthafuckin' abortion clinic calling my gotdamn phone to do a follow-up about an appointment that I knew nothing about?" Yakhi yelled.

Cyber's eyes dropped down to his balled-up fists at his side.

"Why are you here?"

"Bruh, real shit, don't fucking get smart wit' me. Fuck is ya bald headed ass doing down at the abortion clinic' bruh?"

Looking up at him with innocent eyes, she replied, "Why do you people go to the abortion clinic?"

"Bitch! Keep playing wit' me."

"You don't have to call me out of my name. You asked a rather dumb question, so I gave you a dumb answer."

"You didn't answer my muthafuckin' question, Cyber. Keep trying to be cute, bruh."

"I am cute, but what is it that I can help you with?"

"Ya ass wanna help a nigga? How about you explain this shit to—,""Fuck that shit, stand the fuck up!" He yelled, yanking her up by the arm.

"Yakhi, get ya fucking hands off me!" She yelled, trying to free her wrist from his hold.

"Naw, fuck that, let me see ya tummy," he said, reaching for the front of her shirt.

Cyber's hands blocked the front of her shirt, while he tried to touch her stomach.

"Leave me alone, Khi. Take your ass back to Michigan and go lay up and create a bunch of babies with that ugly ass, tooth fairy looking bitch, you playing house with."

"Fuck you! So, because I moved on, you take ya funky ass to the clinic to kill my seed? You one cold hearted bitch, man," Yakhi stated, as the tremble in his voice started to change. "Let me see your stomach, ma," he said as he closed the distance between them.

Out of nowhere, her nipples hardened. She had become aroused at his vulnerability. It didn't matter though, because she had no intention to go back down that road with him. Cyber finally decided to put him out of his misery and let him check her stomach.

"Why ya stomach so hard, just in that one spot?"

"Because, jerk off, that's where the baby is curled up at." His eyes left her stomach and jerked up toward her face.

"You didn't kill my baby?"

Cyber shook her head no and smiled internally as he sat on his shins in the middle of her apartment and talked to him or her through her belly.

"If you didn't kill my baby, why they call talking about a follow-up appointment?"

"Because I wanted to mind fuck you, like you did me," she said, swatting his hands off her rather round behind.

Cyber walked over to the couch and sat down. It was never her plan to kill their child. She purposely gave the clinic his number because she was being spiteful, knowing that they would call. Cyber wasn't cut like that. She wasn't going to do something that would change her life forever, or change the way she viewed herself, because she couldn't take rejection.

"I wanna apologize to you about that shit. So much shit has been going on, a nigga should've known you wouldn't fold on me."

"There's no need to apologize. I don't accept your apology because it wasn't genuine. Somewhere deep inside of you, you think that I did set you up. I would never do some shit like that to you, but you obviously don't know me by now, so there's no need to fake the funk."

He walked over to her and leaned down. Placing his lips softly on her forehead, he kissed her gently and then grabbed her hands. Pulling her up on her feet, he scooped her up as if he was carrying his newborn baby and carried her to her bedroom.

Because her apartment was only a one bedroom, it

didn't take Yakhi long to find her bedroom. He walked in and laid her down on the bed. He climbed up on the bed and grabbed her foot, rubbing the pads of her toes, earning a light, muffled moan from her.

"I just want to ask this question and then I'll leave the shit alone." He paused briefly and then proceeded with his question. "When the police asked you if you knew who was responsible for me being shot, did you tell them that you didn't know who did it?"

Cyber shut her eyes tightly as she held her breath. She was hoping he would've left the question alone, she didn't want to lie to him. And by the same token, she didn't want to tell him the truth either. Getting out of her head, she realized too much time had lapsed since he finished his sentence and she knew she had to say something—but what?

"There was a lot of shit going on that night. I spoke to multiple people that night. I'm not sure who I spoke to. They all kept asking me did I know who did it and—,"

"Just answer the question," he said lowly.

"I—I did tell them I didn't know who shot you." She sucked in a huge breath and closed her eyes, as water rushed down her face.

The room was silent. Both caught up in their own thoughts, that they didn't speak on, neither knew what to say. Yakhi stopped rubbing her foot and placed it on the edge of the mattress. Standing to his feet, he walked out of her room, through the hallway and to the front door.

Before he could get out of the door good, he felt her pulling on the back of his jacket. Turning around he looked up at her.

"I was trying to protect the both of you. In my own stupid and selfish way, I wasn't trying to be just another person she dealt with that had turned their back on her. I was confused then, but I'm not confused now. I know where my loyalty lies. A week after the shooting, I went into the police station and gave an official statement. I went to turn her in, but the officers informed me that they had already found her dead body. I went to turn her in, not because I was trying to keep you from finding out, but because it was the right thing to do and I'm riding with you right or wrong," she said and then closed the door behind him.

Cyber knew that he would eventually find out. It was just like the old saying, what's done in the dark always comes to the light. She knew that he would've automatically assumed that she was protecting Layah because she was still in love with her and wanted to secretly be back with her. Which wasn't totally true. Yes, Cyber did love Layah, but there was a big difference between loving someone and being in love with someone. She loved the history that they had. She loved the way Layah treated her in the beginning of their relationship, when things were still fresh and dewy. But that was were the love ended. Yakhi came and swept her up in this thugged out ass romance,showing her how to value and appreciate herself.

So, she knew that her disloyalty would be questioned and that he wouldn't want shit to do with her. She expected that to happen, and she couldn't fault him for viewing her differently. If the shoe was on the other foot, her head would've spun into a complete circle exorcist style. She climbed up into her bed and prayed that one day Yakhi would find it in his heart to forgive her. She wouldn't hold her breath while chewing bubble gum, waiting on that day to come, though.

27

YAKHI

Loyal to The Thought of Us But My Heart Steady Screaming Fuck You

Yakhi sat in the front room of his hotel room, blowing on an ounce of Gorilla Glue, in his feelings. He had just left Cyber's place when she admitted that she lied to everyone about who shot him. The shit was bothering him so bad, he kept having nightmares. Whoever came up with the saying 'the truth hurts' was spot on because Yakhi wasn't ready for her truth. He didn't know if it was because he felt like he wouldn't ever really have all of her, or if it was because she was protecting the bitch who did everything in her power to tear down her self-esteem.

Tossing the lighter across the table, Yakhi slid down the couch cushions, pissed that he was still allowing her presence to roam around freely in his mind. He ran his hands down his face and then sat up, grabbing the remote control to the 55" flat screen that was mounted to the wall. He turned the channel to Sports Center and tried to focus on the basketball game between the Los Angeles Lakers and the Boston Celtics. After pretending to be interested in the game for five minutes, he turned the television off and sat back against the couch. He was so fucking bored that he didn't know what to do. He wanted to hit up the club, but he didn't know shit about South Carolina's social scene. And even if he did, he didn't feel like being bothered.

The urge to go back to her house and cuddle up with her, while he rubbed her belly, feeling his son squirm around, was super strong. Just thinking about her carrying his seed put a smile on his face. The idea of having a kid never crossed his mind, but now that he knew that he was having one, he was super excited to be a father.

Yakhi didn't have a great relationship with his own father. He always felt like his father, Samuel, was in competition with him. Like if his mother doted on him, his dad would step in and tell her that she was femininizing him. It had gotten so bad that Racquel stopped showing him affection altogether.

Yakhi was convinced that it was his father that told her to stop, and that was the reason for his rebellion against his parents. He vowed to be a better man and role model to his son or daughter. He was secretly praying that Cyber was carrying twins. He wanted his kid to have a sibling.

Someone they could be close to and tell all their secrets to, like he did with Yakhiyah.

It was his last day in SC and he had finally found clarity. Yakhi concluded that he couldn't continue to pursue a marriage with Cyber. What she did really hurt him, and he couldn't trust her. The next best thing was to be supportive of the rest of her pregnancy and then to co-parent once the babies came. The night before, he kept having dreams that she was carrying twins, two little boys who looked just like him. Until he was told otherwise, he would continue to assume that she was giving him two bad ass little boys.

Yakhi was on his way to the airport, with his bags in his hand. When he opened the door, he was stunned to see Cyber standing outside his room door. He was confused and a little irritated that she knew where he was staying, but you couldn't tell by the way his eyes traced her silhouette several times.

"What you doing here?" He asked, dropping his bags to the floor.

"I have a doctor's appointment, and I wanted to see if you wanted to come?"

He scoffed at her explanation. He was trying to keep his cool, but his patience with her was wearing thin.

"You hid seven and a half months' worth of appointments from me, so why is this appointment so important?"

"I did keep the pregnancy from you for my own reasons. I didn't know if I wanted to be with you or not. You have to understand, I went from being with a woman for most of my life, and then one day I meet a guy that had the ability to do what so many others couldn't. And that was capture my attention. I had never cheated on Layah before, and the shit happened effortlessly. So, I apologize for running out on you. I wasn't ready then."

"You weren't ready, but you damn sure didn't turn me down when we ran to Vegas and got married though."

"In my defense, I didn't know we were going to Vegas, much less to get married. I never said I wasn't feeling you, I just wasn't used to being with a man. You made me feel wanted, like I was worthy of the moon and the stars. You seemed genuine in your pursuit to get my attention and my time. And even though I was in a relationship, I fell in love with you."

Yakhi tried to tune out the sound of her voice. He pretended to be enthralled with the people who were walking to and from their rooms, just so she didn't think she was pulling him back in.

"Yakhi, I'm sorry," she said as she reached for his arm.

Yakhi pulled away from her, grabbed his bags and, headed down the hallway.

"Hurry the fuck up so I can get the fuck away from you, bruh!" He called out over his shoulder.

The two of them sat in a cold, sterile room with tons of equipment, as they waited on her doctor to show up. The room was unusually quiet, and he could tell Cyber was getting antsy. He kept his eyes down on his phone screen, but every so often, he could see her knees shaking out of his peripheral view.

"Are you excited?" She asked, breaking the silence.

"Naw," he said in a disinterested tone.

"I am. Do you want a girl or a boy?" She asked.

"Don't matter, long as he or she is healthy."

Cyber blew out a frustrated breath. She was getting pissed that he was acting that way. She was hoping that him coming to see their baby would help bring him around, but he was making it very difficult.

Knock. Knock. Knock.

"Is it okay if I come in?" The voice asked from the other side of the door.

"Yes." She half-yelled. She was officially over the day. Yakhi had come and sucked the fun right out of the situation, and now she was irritated and wanted to get away from him.

"So, are you ready to know the gender, daddy?" Doctor McCormick asked, as she put on a pair of gloves.

Cyber looked over at Yakhi, but he was so engrossed in his phone that he didn't even hear her.

"Yakhi!"

"What's up?" He said coolly.

"The doctor was talking to you, you're being very rude," Cyber fussed.

"Don't take me there, ma," he said lowly.

"Can we hurry this up please?" Cyber said, on the verge of tears.

Doctor McCormick nodded her head and then assisted Cyber backward on the white paper that was standard in any doctor's office. Placing the cold blue jelly on the ultrasound transducer, she then applied it to her hard and swollen belly. She slid the probe across the top of her abdomen and held it in place for a few minutes. The once silent room was filled with the sound of a heartbeat.

Yakhi couldn't help the smile that popped on his face. He pushed the button on the side of his Samsung Galaxy Note 10, making the screen go black. He sat up in his chair and closed his eyes as he listened to the distorted sounds that filled the speaker on the ultrasound machine.

"Hey, doc, can you place the thingy on the bottom of her stomach to the right?"

Doctor McCormick looked over her shoulder at him and then back down to Cyber's stomach. Doing as he asked, she placed the transducer on the bottom right hand side of her belly, and she felt a kick. Her eyes jilted to the screen and her eyes narrowed in slits. Frantically, she moved the probe back to the top of her stomach, then off to the side, and that's when she saw it. Yakhi just held his head down and waited for confirmation on his hunch.

"Is there something wrong, doctor?" Cyber asked, feeling alarmed. She had been watching the doctor's facial expressions ever since Yakhi asked his request.

"Umm, yes and no. No, because the news isn't bad, and

yes, because I don't know how we missed this, but there appears to be two fetuses in the womb," Doctor McCormick said.

"There's what?" She sat up confused.

"We're having twins, ma," Yakhi said quietly.

"How—how did we miss this?"

"Well, it's actually quite common for one baby to hide behind the other. So, when we did the exam, we were only seeing one fetus."

"Well, is the second baby alright?"

"Lay back for me please?" The doctor asked.

Doing as she was told, Cyber laid back on the white paper and watched as the two sacs appeared on the small monitor. Tears immediately rushed to the forefront of her retinas. Her heart was beating so fast, she thought the poor thing was going to explode.

"Baby B is fine. Would you two like to know the sex?" She asked, as she poured more gel on the transducer.

"Yes," They said at the same time.

Placing the probe back onto her belly, she moved it around a few more times and then started typing on the mini keyboard that was in the middle of the machine.

"Okay, I want you to schedule another appointment at the hospital to check on their growth. Since this new development has arisen, I'm going to schedule you to be induced one month from now, if everything is alright from the test. Have you been doing your NST's?"

"Yes, ma'am."

"Okay, here are your pictures and a wash cloth for you stomach. Congratulations you two." She handed Cyber the pictures and started to wipe down the equipment. When she was finished, she walked out of the room.

Cyber sat up on the bed, wiping the cold jelly off her belly. Neither of them said a word. When she was done, she opened the folded-up piece of paper and stared at the words. More tears saturated her face as she passed the pictures over to Yakhi. She stood to her feet, grabbed her jacket and her purse and walked out the room.

Yakhi looked down at the words, and he just chuckled. He wanted to say that he knew all along, but he didn't. Thinking back, he did notice that his appetite had really picked up, and that was before Cyber showed up the second time. He just shrugged it off as the streets stressing him and then the whole situation with Cyber in itself. Then there was the inkling that she was having twins. He just chucked that up as his twintuition. The thought to check the right side of her belly came to him from the many times his mother told him and Yakhiyah about her experience when she found out she was having twins. Initially, she thought it was just one baby, but Yakhiyah was hiding down on the bottom right side of her stomach as well.

Yakhi picked his phone up from his lap, snapped a photo of the ultrasound and sent it to Yakhiyah and his mother. His caption read: *"What the f we gone do with two smaller versions of me?"*

Standing to his feet, he walked out the door and made his way up to the counter where Cyber was standing, talking to the receptionist. Walking up behind her, he wrapped both of his arms around her waist. Leaning forward, he pulled her by the long ponytail that was hanging down her back. With her head bent back, he leaned up into the crook of her neck. He placed his lips an inch away from her ear.

Yakhi opened his mouth and whispered to her. "Thank you, baby." He placed a small kiss on her helix and then stepped back.

Cyber looked over her shoulder and smiled at him. Just seeing her smile was enough to settle his nerves. That was the first time in his life he could say that he was truly happy. Nothing in the world could compare to that feeling; not the money from the streets, not the different bitches riding his dick or the clout he gained for being one of the toughest niggas slanging White in the D

28

NESSIAH

One of The Hardest Decisions

Nessiah was sitting on her lounger on her lanai, talking to her wedding planner, Cyber and Yakhiyah. They were putting the finishing touches on the wedding that was set to take place the next night. It was Qaseem who decided that he wanted to bump the wedding date up, so what was supposed to be an engagement totaling two years and a half, was seven months in length. Nessiah felt like he only wanted to push the wedding up because Dominick was still sniffing around. But she had to own that one, he had decided to leave her alone. And her fast ass invited that man over to her hotel suite and let him take the precious gift, she was supposed to have given her husband to unwrap on their honeymoon.

Ever since that night, Nessiah was trying to hold it together. She was acting like a fucking junkie. He could be in the middle of working at the bar or drawing up different design conceptions for F8, and she would demand that he stopped what he was doing to meet up with her for a passionate quickie. What was supposed to had been one night of magical passion ended up being four nights filled with love, lust and lies.

Dominick: I need to see you A.S.A.P.

Nessiah: I can't, I'm in the middle of something.

Nessiah slid her phone on the side of her leg and tried to pay attention to the things they were discussing, but it was hard with temptation lurking around the corner.

Dominick: I don't really give a fuck about what you're doing. I need to see you right now!

Nessiah: Dominick, you're not calling the shots, I am. And besides, I think we need to chill out on meeting up. I'm trying to take my relationship seriously with him and I can't do that if I'm constantly lying to him.

Dominick: So, you want me to pop up at your house is what you're saying? I already know you're secretly planning your wedding behind my back. Funny how I found out,better yet, it's funny how you never mentioned it as well. You have one hour or I'm popping up at your fucking house. I suggest you wrap up whatever the fuck you're working on and get here NOW!

Nessiah's eyes bugged out of her skull as she read the message on her screen. Her mind had gotten the best of her as she tried to figure out how the hell, he knew she was planning her wedding. She purposely didn't mention it because she didn't know what the hell, he was capable of doing when he did find out. She didn't want him ruining her wedding like he had done his own. She blinked and then went down memory lane. The vivid pictures of what happened at his wedding played rapidly like a PowerPoint presentation on fast forward.

"Nessiah. are you alright?" Delores asked.

"Nessiahhhhh!" Cyber yelled, as she nudged her in the shoulder.

"I'm sorry, what were you saying?"

"That your ass ain't paying us no damn attention," Yakhiyah said, looking at her like she was crazy.

Cyber's eyes dropped down to Nessiah's lap and she saw the messages on her screen. Shaking her head, she grabbed the phone and handed it to Yakhiyah.

"Cyber, don't do that. Hiyah, give me my phone back," Nessiah said, trying to reach over the table.

"Umm, Delores, can you give us a minute really quick, please?"

Not saying another word, Delores stood to her feet, collecting her belongings, walked back through Nessiah's house and headed into the living room to give the women some privacy.

"Really, bitch?" Cyber turned and asked as soon as Delores departed the patio.

"Cyber, don't even start, I have enough shit on my plate. I don't need your judgmental ass comments," Nessiah said, rolling her eyes.

"First off, bitch, don't catch an attitude with me

because ya ass doing dirt and you feeling guilty, no cap. What you are doing doesn't make you any better than Dominick. I'm telling you this because I've grown to like ya bald headed ass. I look at you like a little sister and as your big sister, I'm going to tell you when you wrong, bitch," she said, slapping her on her exposed thigh.

Nessiah put her head down and started to cry. It wasn't her intention to dog Qaseem out. She wasn't still hung up on what he did five years ago and wanted revenge. But things just happened. She had no idea that she would meet someone like Dominick and get herself caught up in a situation like the one she was in.

"If it's that serious between you and him, why not just be with him?" Yakhiyah asked.

That was probably the same question a lot of you were wondering and the answer to that question was that she would've felt like she was diminishing her value. That and he was still communicating with his fiancée. The last time they were together, Arlyse called while they were in the middle of fooling around. Dominick didn't answer the call, but to know that he was still dealing with her pissed Nessiah off, so she left.

"Give me my phone." She stretched her hand across the table and grabbed her phone out of Yakhiyah's hand.

She sat back in her seat and then opened her text messages. She started typing and then exited out of their messages.

Nessiah: *I'll be there in two hours.*

29

QASEEM

There's a Stranger in My House

Qaseem stood with a double shot glass full of whiskey on the rocks, in front of his large picture window, overlooking the large Olympian swimming pool in his backyard. He watched as the steam rose from the water. He loved that the pool came with a heated water feature. The blue and red lights that were implanted along the edge of the yard gave off a calming feel. He watched as Nessiah swam lap after lap, until she was ready to get out.

That had been her thing for the past few weeks. She would come over, swim for a half hour and then come in and go straight to bed. They hadn't talked much since he told her that he didn't want to wait until 2020 to get married. Her reaction wasn't one that he was anticipating, but she readily agreed after some oral persuasion.

If Qaseem would've known that their relationship would've taken such a drastic direction, he wouldn't have suggested that they not wait to marry. In her defense, the wedding planning was stressing her out. He had saw a few of her sketches and the girl was not only gifted, but her visions were innovative. The way she designed her wedding dress, it was hard finding a dress maker who could execute her vision. And lets not mention the way she wanted to decorate the venue had become very stressful.

He had long ago told her to get a wedding planner to plan the entire event, she hired Delores to "help", but she wouldn't allow the poor woman to do anything. That was one of the things he admired about her. She was always so determined to pull things off and make everyone happy.

He snapped out of his thoughts as he watched her step out the pool. Drying her body off, she headed toward the sliding glass door. She was startled upon seeing him standing in front of the window. It wasn't her intention to run into him. She stood there drying her hair, as they stared at each other. Qaseem opened the door and she started toward him.

"Hey," she mumbled quietly.

"Hey, how was your swim?" He asked, as he stepped back to allow her space to walk into the guest bedroom.

"I just had a lot on my mind. I didn't mean to interrupt you."

"Why would you think that?"

"I'm just saying, I did pop up over here uninvited," she said as she walked into the bathroom to take off the wet swimsuit she had on.

Qaseem stood in the doorway, with his head resting against the wooden frame. He exhaled softly as his eyes closed.

"What's bothering you?"

"Why do you ask that?" She said as her heart started to beat faster.

"You've been so distant lately and not to mention, you only come over here to swim. You told me once before that you loved to swim, and it helped you sort your thoughts out when you weren't capable of doing it on solid ground."

Nessiah rolled her eyes as she thought that she talked too damn much. It was okay to keep some things to yourself.

"It's just everything with the wedding. I swear if I knew how to do some of the things I wanted for the venue, I would just do the shit myself," she said the first thing that came to her mind.

Her eyes dropped down to the floor as she thought about how much she'd been lying lately. It wasn't the fact that she was lying, but more so to do with the fact that it came so easily. Her head lifted up and she stared at herself in the mirror, she barely recognized herself. Her eyes squinted as she assessed herself. What was jaw dropping was that she didn't feel bad for letting Dominick take her virginity. She felt like he deserved it, —and Qaseem deserved her heart. Just thinking about Dominick had her clutching her thighs together, wishing that she would've met up with him like she said she would.

"Babe that's why you have a wedding planner. Utilize her so you don't have to bare the load of stress."

"Well, luckily the wedding is tomorrow, then I won't have all of this stress on me. And I'll go back to being your good girl." She smiled at that thought. Getting a clean slate once they said 'I Do' was what she promised herself. She had no interest in fucking around on him. She had basically sown her wild oats so to speak.

"I want to see your face, Ne."

"Babe, you know we're not supposed to see each other the night before the wedding. How was your bachelor party?"

"It was okay, I wasn't really feeling it. Too busy worried about you."

"Why were you worried about me? I'm okay, Qa."

"I don't know. To be honest, for the past month, I've been having dreams of you leaving me at the altar," He mumbled quietly.

Tears welled up in her eyes because she didn't want to put him through so much pain. Wondering if the woman who said she would love you for better or worst deciding not to honor that vow had to be heartbreaking.

"I won't leave you at the altar, Qa," she whispered.

"Please don't!" He said, walking away from the bathroom door. As he closed the bedroom door, he said a prayer to God.

"Please bring back the woman I fell in love with. If there's any doubt in her mind, please ease it, Jesus. I really love her. In Jesus name, amen."

30

NESSIAH

The Day She Gave Her Heart Away

The night time breeze blew in her face, blowing her curls behind her shoulders. The day she had always dreamed of was finally here. Ever since she was seven or closer to eight years old, she would have the same dream every night. Nessiah even went to the extreme to write down every detail. Every night and just like clockwork in every dream, some new detail was added. It wasn't until she turned twelve, that she finally walked down the aisle.

She spent four long years building the perfect wedding. So naturally, when Qa asked her to marry him, she didn't need to go out and get a bunch of expensive magazines to cut pictures from, because she already knew every detail. The real task was finding everything on her list. That was why she was adamant about not hiring a wedding planner, but she did it to ease the tension between her and Qaseem.

In her dream, she pictured herself in a big mansion on a hill overlooking the Persia Gulf. The winding trail from her bedroom window would be covered in pink and white rose petals after all her guest made their way to the pavilion that would be set up on the beach. The flaps on both ends of the tent would be pulled back with twine to allow the Persian breeze to bless their flawless skin. The inside of the tent would be decorated in the prettiest, silkiest, blushing bride pink and ivory, hanging from the rafters inside the huge tent, fairy strip lamps with lights luminating their name and special date in pink and white bulbs. Every chair would be made of golden bamboo, with the top of the chairs draped in ivory silk bows. A long train in the same coordinating pink would also be covered in pink and white rose petals.

A smile covered her face as she thought about how she pulled off her dream wedding. When Cyber and Yakhiyah first asked what the theme for the wedding was, she hesitated because she didn't want them thinking she was crazy for remembering every detail from a series of dreams that took place over 15 years ago. And just like she expected, that's exactly what Cyber said, Yakhiyah, on the other hand, thought that it was romantic.

A knock to her bedroom door distracted her thoughts. She turned around on her Moroccan pouffe, as Yakhiyah and Cyber poked their heads through the cracked door.

"Girl, why the hell do you have this chain on the door like this?" Hiyah asked.

Standing to her feet, she headed to the door and opened it, blessing Yakhiyah with a kiss on the cheek.

"Her ass probably up in here smoking crack," Cyber said, with her nose turned up.

Nessiah swatted her on the ass as she walked passed.

"You better be so lucky ya ass is damn near about to explode, because I started to kick ya in the ass crack."

They all cracked up laughing, as she took her rightful place on her foot stool, overlooking the views down below.

"So, is Rapunzel ready for her journey down the aisle?" Cyber asked.

Nessiah smiled at the analogy to the story of Rapunzel. Here she was in this huge mansion, holed up in a room on the highest floor. Her naturally long hair had added extensions in them that graced the top of her big ole butt. The irony was laughable.

"Yes, but I must admit, I am nervous," she said as she placed her index finger in her mouth. The thought of her messing up the gel manicure she'd gotten hours earlier, had her removing her fingers from between her teeth.

"What are you nervous about?" Hiyah asked.

"I don't know. For some strange reason, I just have a bad feeling," she said as she closed her eyes and tried to calm the fluttering from the 'butterflies' in the pit of her stomach.

"It's just cold feet, babe. You'll be just fine as soon as

you step foot on that aisle," Cyber said, getting up to rub her shoulders.

"But, I just feel like I'm not good enough for him now."

"What do you mean now? Now that you're not a virgin anymore?" Yakhiyah asked for clarification.

Instead of responding, she simply nodded her head.

"Nessiah, don't do that. You can't do that poor man like that. Your ass is getting married to-damn-day, even if I have to drag ya ass down that damn aisle by those tracks in ya head," Cyber said, applying pressure to her shoulder blades.

"Ouch! Damn, Cyber. Shred my damn skin with those long ass cat nails, why don't cha?" She said, pushing her hands from her shoulder blades.

"I'm with Cy. Why would you wait until the day of your wedding to be having second thoughts?"

"Okay, first off, who said anything about calling off the wedding? I just said I didn't feel worthy of his love, and y'all went ahead and jumped the gun," Nessiah said, rolling her eyes.

"Well, we're just trying to look out for you best interest, but you making the shit impossible while you all in your fucking feelings," Yakhiyah said, rolling her eyes next.

"My best interest, or his? Look I appreciate it, but y'all starting to make the shit repetitive to the point where I don't even want to confide in y'all. Like, for once I just want someone to be on my side, —to see where I'm coming from. I've never dealt with these kinds of feelings."

I've never been mixed up in a situation like this. Like, dawg, I'm in love with the man of my dreams, but society and my morals say I can't have him. And then there's Qa, the first man to ever break my heart, pops back up then comes and mends the damage from the past and the present. I'm conflicted as hell and y'all smart ass remarks ain't helping shit!" Nessiah shouted, as she made her dramatic exit into the ensuite.

TWO HOURS HAD COME and gone, and Nessiah was still held up in the bathroom. Her wedding was set to start in the next twenty minutes, and she was dressed only in a silk nightie, the same one she'd had on since she awakened at the crack of dawn. She stood there in the mirror, just staring at herself. She didn't know what she was trying to find, but she continued to stand in that one spot, staring into her dark, brown eyes. Eyes that once held so much pain, now held love mixed with confusion. For once, Nessiah was being selfish and thinking of herself. She didn't feel guilty about trying to experience something so foreign to her. She wouldn't allow herself to. She felt as if she owed herself those impromptu moments of sin. For once in her life, she wanted to experience what all the other women her age engaged in. Sure, she was set to get married, but the idea came to her before Qaseem had mentioned pushing the date up. Furthermore, she didn't want to experience her first time with him. She wanted Dominick.

Knock. Knock.

"Honey, what are you doing in there?" Her mother asked, tapping on the door with her knuckle.

"I'll be right out," she said, eyes never leaving the mirror.

"Just show me what you want me to see," she mumbled to herself.

After standing there for a few more minutes, she noticed nothing, so she turned around and twisted the knob to turn on the shower. Stripping from her solace, she stepped into the walk-in stall and began to wash her body quickly.

Cyber, Yakhiyah, Nessiah's mother Nirvanna and Delores all stood in a semi-circle as they waited for her to come out the bathroom. The door slowly creaked, and out she came in an all-white dress. The detail in the dress was simple, she had 3\4 quarter sleeves, to hide the fat on her arms. She had a light touch of crystals and beading work on the front and sides of the dress, and then there was the train.

The train on the dress was what really captured her attention and would surely do the same to everyone else. It weighed 2.602 kg and it was shaped like the shell of an Oyster. The dress was an exact replica of her personality; sweet yet simple with a hint of elegance. She watched as her friends and her mother cried tears of joy.

"Oh my God, honey, you look absolutely stunning, — radiant even," her mother complimented.

"Yasss, bish! My bish badd looking like a bag of money, She closed her eyes tight, envisioning every single detail that helped her made a consensus decision." Cyber said, further hyping her up.

"Sis, you look amazing," Yakhiyah said, hugging her as she neared her in the middle of the room.

All Nessiah could do was smile and soak up the attention. She wasn't used to people applauding the way she looked, and it showed by the brightened white smile she couldn't take off display.

"Thanks, you guys. So, what time is it?" She asked slipping her feet into her sliver Swarovski crystal embellished Daffodile pumps made by Christian Louboutin.

"Time to get you out of this room and into the arms of your prince charming," Cyber said, winking at her.

The women gathered their things and headed to the beach where the ceremony was due to take place. As she placed one foot in front of the other, she got an uncomfortable feeling in the middle of her chest. Her head turned from one direction to the next, but nothing out of the ordinary had captured her attention.

Just as she reached the top of the aisle, the soulful sounds of Case's *'Happily Ever After'* serenaded their family and friends. Nessiah smiled as she looped her left arm with her father's and began her journey to her dreams. As they walked to the beat, her father leaned over and whispered in her ear.

"I have never been more proud of you than I am right now."

Tears prickled her Fovea. She was so happy that her father saw her getting married as an accomplishment. So many women miss out on the opportunity to be tied to someone they love for the rest of their lives. That's not to say that it is entirely the women's fault, but about 85% of the blame can be placed on the woman. Instead of standing up for our true value and self-worth, we diminish it by allowing the men in our lives to place us at the standard he feels we should be categorized in, just so he can "have the milk, without purchasing the cow". If we stop allowing ourselves to only be around to provide him with a certain sensation, more women would be wives instead of baby mama's, THOTS and bitter women in general.

"I must say that you make one beautiful bride, and Qaseem is the luckiest man on planet Earth," Messiah Edwards said, as he leaned over and kissed his daughter on the cheek.

"Thanks, daddy," she whispered to him.

As they stopped just in front of the altar, the music ceased and the pastor smiled brightly at Nessiah.

"Who gives this beautiful woman to this man?" Pastor Celeste Armstead asked.

"We do," Messiah and Nirvanna Edwards said.

"Dear friends and family, we are gathered here today to

witness and celebrate the union of Qaseem Maten and Nessiah Edwards in marriage. In all the years they've known each other, there was a strain keeping them from one another, but God saw fit to bring them together again. Since they've been together, their love and understanding of each other has grown and matured, and now they have decided to live their lives together as husband and wife. True marriage begins well before the wedding day, and the efforts of marriage continue well beyond the ceremony's end. A brief moment in time and the stroke of a pen are all that is required to create the legal aspect and bond of a marriage, but it will take a lifetime of love, commitment, and compromise to make a marriage work until the very end. Today you two have decided to declare your commitment here in front of all your family and friends. Your union will only grow with strength and beauty, as as you two fight and work together. With that being said, is there anyone here in the audience who thinks that these two shouldn't be joined together in holy matrimony?"

Nessiah turned toward their guests and there wasn't a word spoken amongst them. Just as she was about to turn around, she spotted him sitting in the third row next to her aunts and a few of her cousins. Nessiah stood there frozen. His face held a stoic expression, one that wasn't easy to decipher. Her heart started galloping in her chest, at the thought of him standing to his feet and calling her out for being the dirty little slut she was. But, he did nothing, said nothing. He just stared at her. Every time he exhaled, her heart started to cry. The situation was so sad. She didn't want their relationship to have taken a messy turn the way it did, but he left her no choice. All he had to do was cut ties with Arlyse, but he wouldn't. And that thought was what made her tear her eyes from his and turn around to face the pastor. Nessiah had to get back to her life. She couldn't be stuck forever in limbo because of his sick ass family "business deal".

"Qaseem informed me that he'd taken time to write his vows, so he will go first and then Nessiah will have her turn."

Qaseem cleared his throat and took both of her hands into his.

"Nessiah, I remember the first time I saw you, it was junior year and, I had just transferred to Romulus high. I didn't know anybody, and I think I stayed to myself for that first week. Then it was as if everyone noticed me. Within the next week, I had become one of the popular kids. I started to get used to the attention from the girls. I had pretty much slept with over half of the females in the sophomore and junior class, within four months of being there. That had gotten old rather quickly. You were one of the smartest girls in my Cal two class senior year. While every girl threw themselves at me, you didn't bat an eye at me. Hell, you didn't even speak to me. I'm not going to lie, that was one of the things that intrigued me about you. I had made up my mind to approach you senior year, but you beat me to the punch, by asking me could you take me to the prom," he said, winking his eye at her.

Qaseem purposely left out the fact that she offered him cash to take her to the prom, because he didn't want to embarrass her in front of their families.

"I messed up that day in the hallway, and I never got over the shit I did to you. It fucked with me tremendously, and I'm just glad that you gave me the opportunity to fix your broken heart. I'm sorry, baby, and I'll spend the rest of my life making you happy. I promise to never hurt you again, like I did that day in the hallway."

Nessiah wiped the tears from her face and then looked over her shoulder. Dominick had just stood to his feet on his way out the tent, when their eyes met. Two seconds later and then he was gone. She turned back around and spoke from her heart, sealing their union.

"Qaseem, you've brought so much joy and happiness in my life. I never thought that I would've experienced this level of happiness. You didn't have to come back into my life and try to fix the damage between us, but you did, and it means the world to me. I am so happy, and I can't wait to become Mrs. Qaseem Lord Maten."

Everyone cheered for Mr. and Mrs. Qaseem Lord Maten, as they made their way down the beach and to the limousine that was parked outside of the mansion, waiting to take them to their Caribbean destination for the next thirty days.

NESSIAH SMILED as their chariot whisked them down the long winding roads of Varadero. She closed her eyes and enjoyed the breeze that smacked her in the face, sending her curls flying to the front of her face and over her shoulders at every turn. Nessiah squeezed her eyelids together and thanked God for allowing her to experience true happiness. Reaching into her purse, she pulled out the pink letterhead from the Air BNB that they stayed at when they first arrived on the Hicacos Peninsula. She titled the letter and let the fine ball point pen glide across the glossy laminated paper.

Dear Dominick,

Thank you for sacrificing your happiness for mine.

~Nessiah

EPILOGUE

Yakhiyah & Saafiq
   We Found Love
   One Year Later....
   "Can I be that?"
   "Be what Saa-baby?"
   "The nigga that makes you smile when you first wake up and go back to bed, for the rest of your life?"
   Yakhiyah stood there in the middle of the ballroom at the Rooster Tail banquet hall in Detroit, with tears in her eyes. When her day started that morning, she didn't have the slightest idea that she would be staring at all their friends and family members, while Saafiq stood before her with a pastor, ready to seal their union for real. She thought that they would've been engaged for longer than they were, especially since they hit that dry patch.
   Who knew that with a past as rocky as theirs, they

would be there in that moment, together? Yakhiyah cupped her big round belly. At just four months pregnant, she looked like she would explode at any moment. It was actually all because of her belly that they were standing there together.

Shortly after they'd reconciled, he went back to his old ways; the late nights, drugs and a dozen women frolicking behind him. Yakhiyah stuck it out for as long as she could before she called it quits. After two long months, and a drunken late night slip up, she found out she was pregnant. When she told him, he did everything in his power to fix his mistakes. He finally got his shit together, and she took him back with the stipulation that it would surely be the last time.

"I couldn't imagine spending the rest of my life with anyone but you!" She shouted, as she leaned up and kissed him on the lips.

"Well, I guess there's only one thing to say after that. I now pronounce you Mr. and Mrs. Saafiq Harlen Daniels. You may now kiss your bride, again!" The pastor joked.

"Gimmie that tongue nigga!" Saa said.

Yakhiyah shook her head and grabbed the back of his head. Their lips locked once again and everyone in the venue started clapping and cheering the couple on.

SIX MONTHS LATER, they welcomed a beautiful baby girl,

Chance Kadence Daniels. Saafiq and Yakhiyah settled into a new, three-bedroom condominium in Farmington Hills. Who knew that all it would take was a thug to love her beyond all of the pain in her life? Yakhiyah had went her whole life seeking validation from everyone who claimed they loved her. She realized that people can say they love you all day, every day, but if their actions didn't match up, it was just talk.

Saafiq showed her that love was an emotion that had to be shown in order to be rendered useful. Love is unconditional. Love is not supposed to hurt, manipulate or cause harm to a person. His love provided solace. He was the answer to all her prayers.

Shreece

The Road to Hell

While everyone was out living their best life, Shreece was fighting to save her own. The news had a personal vendetta against her. That was the only plausible explanation she could come up with, because every second she turned around, the news was still talking about her trial, even a whole year later. They especially liked to talk about it whenever a small child was murdered. The first six months were hell, If she wasn't fighting herself to just end her life, she had to deal with the other women around her trying to.

Here it was, a whole year later, and she still hadn't adjusted to life in prison. Everything around her was negative; she had lost her will to survive. Shreece didn't waste her time thinking about the good times in her life, because that was when she contemplated suicide the most. Just knowing that she would never be free to roam the streets again or working with sickly children killed the last little bit of her soul.

She was at her wits end, as she laid on her bunk and traced the fat veins that circled her wrist. She had just gotten out of confinement for fighting in the chow hall. She was put in isolation for two weeks for the fight. Just thinking about being cooped up in the darkened cell made her apply pressure to the nail file she had stashed in the hole in the bottom of her mattress.

The splash of blood hit her in the face and a smile a

mile long appeared on her face. The high she got from the loss of blood made her feel like she was floating on air. She was so out of it that she dug deeper into the open vein. After a few minutes, she started shaking then laid back on her cot and closed her eyes as she felt like she was wading on a yacht in the Caribbean.

Time ticked by and by the time shift change came to check on the inmates, the CO was disgusted by the scene in front of her. Shreece's entire bunk and the walls around her was covered in blood. It looked as if someone had doused her and her bunk with a bucket of blood. When CO Green and a few others entered the cell, it was already too late. They shook their head at the sight. No one felt bad; they all agreed that she took the cowardly way out. Most of the Corrections Officers were paying the inmates with extra chow and recreation time to pick on Shreece. They hated baby killers, so they figured someone would kill her, but they didn't expect for her to do the deed herself.

Yakhi & Cyber

Let Go of Love, If It Comes Back It's Yours Forever

Cyber sat back in her seat and wiped the stream of tears from her face, watching her best friend in admiration as Saafiq surprised her with a bomb ass wedding ceremony. She was so excited to see her friend finally happy. Cyber was a shoulder to cry on so many nights for Yakhiyah. She knew that the real reason she refused to date was because she wanted Saafiq. Yakhiyah flat out refused to deal with another man.

Her words verbatim were, *"I'm only interested in pursuing something with my nigga. I don't have the energy to entertain somebody else's dusty ass son. I know when Saa looks at me that he has my best interest at heart. If the shit doesn't work out with him, I'm finish with men for good!"*

So, it was really good to see that they were able to work pass all of their issues, especially with them expecting a baby girl in the next five months.

"Ma-ma up, up, up," Yannis said in his baby voice.

Before she could pick him up, his twin brother, Yasunari, came rushing toward her and his brother on wobbly legs. The twins had just turned one years old earlier in the year, and Cyber couldn't believe that she was a mother. Her boys gave her such a happy, unexplainable feeling. Nothing in the world could compare to the feeling she got waking up every morning and seeing their little hi-yellow faces, who were every bit of Yakhi's twins.

They all looked just alike; like a fucking mini triplet gang, as he called it.

"My bad, I didn't know he would take off like that." Yakhi said, damn near out of breath.

Cyber looked up and smiled at him, but it wasn't a long-lasting smile. As soon as she saw his girlfriend, Amelei, walking up behind him, her smile dropped. Cyber thought for sure that after their doctor visit, they were going to be on the road to regaining each other's trust. He made sure he brought her back and forth to all her appointments after that first one. He made sure she ate and upgraded her little Dodge Caliber to a 2018 Dodge Durango. He was always around and helping her with whatever she needed.

Although he was doing all of that, they were never intimate, he never spent the night and he kept his distance if she didn't need anything. She never made a move on him or tried to bring the topic up, because, in her mind, she thought she was giving him space to be able to trust her again. What she was really doing was opening the door a little bit wider for Amelei to slither her little skinny ass through the crack.

She found it hilarious that he claimed to love her height and her figure, but both Aoki and Amelei were smaller in stature and skinny as hell. He didn't know it, but that only made her that much more insecure. So much so, she shed thirty pounds of her pregnancy weight. When she had first gotten pregnant, she wasn't showing at all, but as soon as she neared the end of her sixth month, she blew up like a water balloon. Having to deal with the extra weight gain and then finding out Yakhi snuck off and found a new girlfriend, was enough to push her over the edge.

If it wasn't for hearing Yannis and Yasunari heartbeat at every appointment, she probably would've committed suicide. So many people are oblivious to depression. They figure if they don't see it or haven't experienced it, it simply doesn't exist. Or they labeled those who suffer from depression as attention seekers, when that's merely not the case. Depression is real, it hits at anytime, and it can affect any race, shape, size and gender. Cyber hid her depression well, since she felt like she had no one to turn to. Even though she had Yakhiyah and Nessiah, who she recently became friends with, she didn't want to throw all her problems onto them, when they had problems of their own.

"Cyber, nice to see you again," Amelei said.

Cyber simply smiled then turned and watched as Yakhiyah and Saafiq slow danced to Avant and Keke Wyatt's rendition of '*My first love*'. Just that quickly,her mood had been dampened. She tried to tune the two out, as they talked about having an event there. Just hearing them discuss doing anything together literally made her stomach turn. So, instead of causing a scene, she stood up and abandoned her seat for one across the room.

She was sitting there minding her own business, when she looked up and noticed Yakhi walking in her direction.

She exhaled rather harshly and then rolled her eyes, as he approached her.

"What's with all that?" He asked, taking the empty seat that was in front of her.

Cyber smiled as she watched Yakhiyah twerking with her baby bump, totally ignoring Yakhi and his statement.

"So, you gone act like you don't hear me talking to you?" He asked, pinching her on her wrist.

"Yakhi, what is it that you want? Don't come over here bothering me," she snapped.

Yakhi turned completely around in the chair with both of his legs on either side of the chair, gaining direct eye contact with her. He sat there just staring at her; there was something so dark and bitter about her. If he didn't know any better, he would've sworn that she was jealous.

"You jealous?" He asked with his eyes squinted.

"Yakhi, leave me the fuck alone!" She screamed out, drawing the attention of everyone else in the room.

Cyber looked around at all the nosy fuckers sitting around watching her and Yakhi. Embarrassed, she grabbed Yannis and Yasunari and walked out the door that lead to the dock where the motorized jets skis were zooming around in the water. She sat down on a lounger with both boys on her legs, watching the adults race one another.

Cyber was sitting there for five minutes, when she heard footsteps behind her. She huffed loudly and started gathering her things to head out.

"Are you okay, sis?" Nessiah asked.

Cyber nodded her head, but as soon as Nessiah wrapped her arms around her shoulder, she burst into tears.

"It's going to be okay, sis, don't cry," Nessiah said as she rubbed small circles on her back.

"Do—do you know that motherfucker had the nerve to ask me was I jealous?"

"Cy, don't—,"

"Well, aren't you?" His deep voice was heard over the buzzing from the motors on the jet skis.

"I'll call you later, Nessiah. Yannie and Ari, let's go." Cyber grabbed their small hands and went to walk around their father, but she didn't get far, because he grabbed up both of the boys by their arms and pulled them into his legs.

"I thought I was getting them for the weekend?" He asked, as his eyes assaulted her body.

"Well, I changed my mind, you can get them next weekend." she said, looking off in the distance. She didn't like the way he was staring at her. To be honest, she was pissed off that he still had that affect on her body. All it took was one look and her entire body flushed with warm goose bumps.

"Naw, you said I had them this weekend, so I'm gone get them this weekend." He said, closing the distance between the two of them.

Nessiah stood back watching the two interact. She

couldn't help but to smile at their aggressive demeanor toward one another. Yakhi slickly palmed the inside of Cyber's thigh out of the view of his sons and the others that were outside that day.

"Fix yo' fucking face, man. You too fucking beautiful to have ya face all frowned up. That jealousy shit is not a good look on you, ma," he said, as he tried to ease his finger inside of her thin, lacy thong.

"Jealous of what? Get the fuck out of here," she said, shoving him out of her space.

"Jealous of the fact that she riding all nine inches of this troublemaker," he said out loud, wit a smirk on his face.

The visual of his skinny ass girlfriend riding her dick triggered something deep inside of her. She blinked once and then lunged at him. Her feet lifted off the ground, and she tackled him down to the dock. Her fists rained punches down on his chest and neck, as her emotions got the best of her.

"Cy, that's enough," Nessiah said, as she tried to yank her off him.

"Yakhiyahhhh!" Nessiah screamed.

Everything happened so fast, she didn't know what to do first. Initially she went to grab her off him, but then she thought about the boys who were standing there watching the fight take place, so she ended up grabbing the boys, and calling for help.

Yakhiyah, Saafiq, Amelei and a few others from Saafiq

and Yakhi's family came rushing out to see what the commotion was. Yakhiyah ran over and snatched Cyber off her brother by the back of her dress.

"What the fuck is wrong with you? Bitch, do you not see my fucking nephew's standing here watching you act like a fucking hood rat?"

"Get your fucking hands off me, Hiyah! I'm sick of this motherfucker. He thinks he can just say whatever the fuck he wants to me, but I'm not going for that shit."

"Shut the fuck up, stupid ass bitch! What the fuck you mad for, huh? You wanna play hurt, but you were the same bitch lying about ya ex shooting me!" Yakhi yelled.

Silence loomed around them, as he fought to refrain from putting his hands on her. The only thing that was saving her was his sons, who were watching him. In his mind, she better had been lucky that they were out there because he most definitely would've hit her ass back.

"You out here acting an ass because he moved on? Get the fuck over it, Cyber. You too got damn grown to be out here with ya ass all out, trying to fight this man, because you fucked up."

Cyber stood upright and looked around at all the faces surrounding them, —feeling embarrassed yet again. Her eyes darted over to Yakhi, only to find Amelei kneeling down, wiping blood from his busted lip. Seeing her trying to nurse his injuries only infuriated her further. Before anyone saw it coming, Cyber ran and attacked Amelei.

Pinning her down to the deck, she slapped that girl

silly. Saafiq didn't move right away, because he wanted her to get all the frustration out. And plus, he wasn't too fond of Amelei, so he took his time peeling Cyber off the girl. Once she was placed on her feet, she grabbed her sons by the hands, raced back inside the venue and out the front entrance.

Several weeks had passed, before Yakhi finally caught up with Cyber and his sons. The first thing he did was back-hand the shit out of her for running off with his kids. After fighting for thirty minutes and tearing her new place apart, they both flopped down on the couch out of breath. Where they sat in silence for several minutes.

"I only got with her to make you jealous," he said suddenly.

Cyber rolled her eyes and continued to stare at the wall in front of her.

"The shit didn't work though. I thought I was gon' get with shorty and she was gon' be the answer to all of my problems, but it only made shit worse between us."

Stubborn, she still refused to address his sudden confession. She was way pass an apology. He had hurt and embarrassed her in front of their family and friends. When she left Yakhiyah's event, she cut ties with all of them. It hurt too much to look all them in the face and relive that day. She looked so pathetic, and she hated herself for playing herself like that.

"So, you ain't got shit to say?" He questioned.

When she didn't respond, he climbed on the floor, crawled over to her and forced his way between her legs.

"Look at me, ma," he said, grabbing her by the chin, forcing her to look at him.

"See, that fucking attitude of yours is the fucking problem. You always feel like you gotta act tough and shit, but what the fuck you gon' learn is that I'm the muthafuckin' man in this here relationship. I run this shit!" He hollered, hitting his closed palm in the middle of his chest.

Cyber sat back against the couch and stared down at him. Their eyes were unmoving as they silently fought for control over the other. Cyber was so used to having to be tough in order to survive, she didn't know how to let go. She wasn't used to being in a relationship with a man. It wasn't hard to relinquish control to Layah, because she demanded it, but Yakhi was different.

Yakhi wasn't aggressive; he was very secure in his manhood. Layah had to pretend to be tough and possess the mindset like a man, whereas it came naturally for Yakhi simply because he was a man.

"I'm not gon' keep having this conversation with you. I'm not gon' beg you to chill and take the back seat and let me handle shit. You gon' do that shit, or I'm gon' stop fucking wit' you. That simple."

Cyber rolled her eyes, but she exhaled a sigh of relief.

She didn't want to lose him. It was quite refreshing to let her guard down and not have to worry about defending herself and her sons. The idea of being in a healthy, stress-free relationship with him was well welcomed.

"Don't you have a girlfriend to get home to?" She said smartly.

"Fuck is my sons at? Get them and tell them daddy's home," he said, walking toward the back of her new condo.

"Yakhi, what time are you going home?"

Stopping in his tracks, he looked over his shoulder at her.

"Fuck, is you slow? Nigga, I just said daddy's home," he said, continuing his stride into what he knew was her bedroom.

Real love hits differently when it comes from someone with a natural schema. Love is not used with ill intentions; real love has no conditions or motives other than to make you smile. So, if you've found love smile, it's a beautiful thing!

Dominick

Living My Truth

Dominick stood against the railing of his Sunseeker KD1900, holding onto the note Nessiah had written him, as his yacht coasted the calm waters in the Caribbean Sea. He admired the beauty that was surrounding him. The dark blues and hues of green made him wish that he didn't feel as if he was there alone. He wished he could've been able to share it with the one woman who was made especially for him. Sadly, that wasn't the case, and never would be.

Dominick knew when Nessiah stood him up the last time he summoned her to meet up with him, it was the end of them. The icing on the cake, was watching her as she cried walking down the aisle. His mind was screaming at him to stand to his feet and ruin her wedding. Like Déjà vu, he saw her turning him down in front of the hundreds of people who were in attendance, just like she did a year ago. That day was the day that humbled everything about him.

Being a man who had everything at his fingertips, he wouldn't hesitate to tell anyone who asked that he'd grown into a cocky son of a bitch. A man who could have any woman his eyes locked on. So it was a deafening defeat when she turned him down. He just knew he'd made a mark on her; he just knew that she would never leave him alone. But she proved him wrong time and time again.

In some ways, he preyed on her weakness for him. He

held the type of power over her that led them both to believe that they were soulmates. Never in his life did he believe in that love at first sight bullshit, but his mind, his heart, and his life would be forever changed by Nessiah Rayne Edwards.

So, because of the stress he put her through, he decided to set her broken heart free. Being a selfish man wouldn't do shit but make him feel worst. Realistically, he couldn't give her what she wanted, so there was no sense in tying her down into a relationship where she wouldn't be happy. He knew that seeing her unhappy would make him feel like shit, so he let her go.

Dominick picked up the half full bottle of E&J VSOP and turned the bottle up to his lips. He guzzled the warm liquor as he tried to drown out his fucked up choices. When there was only a shot, or two worth of alcohol left in the bottle, he pulled the bottle away from his lips. His eyes darted out at the ocean for a few moments. He looked down at the beautiful water that kept crashing against the rear of his boat. The stillness caused an ache so severe, it was hard to catch his breath.

He closed his eyes and laid his forehead on the railing as he focused on the sound of the waves crashing around him. He took small, calm breaths, as he waited for the anxiety attack to pass. He finally stood upright, letting the note fly away with the small breeze. He watched as it flew several feet away from his boat and then landed on the water.

The small ripples took the note further and further away from him. When it was no longer in his sights, he grabbed the bottle and poured the remaining alcohol out into the ocean.

"How much longer are you going to stand out here?" Arlyse asked, coming out on the deck.

"As long as it takes for you to realize that you're not wanted here, and then you pack your shit up and dip," he said, storming past her.

"Dominick, you sound so fucking bitter. Like, get the fuck over it already. The bitch left you for someone else, who she married. What was the point of marrying me, if you were going to continue to mope and cry about her not choosing you?"

Dominick continued into the cabin on his yacht. He wasn't interested in holding a conversation with her any more. Yup, it was true, he did end up marrying her. Their ceremony was nothing like the previous one. That one he'd spent well over a quarter of a million dollars for nothing. The second go-round, he didn't even show up. He simply paid the pastor to print up the marriage certificate and had it mailed to him, which he signed three months later.

Arlyse really believed that deep down he had some love for her somewhere in his hardened chest cavity. But that was all a figment of her imagination. He only married her to keep himself out of prison, since her punk ass father threatened to have him taken into police custody if he didn't. He was starting to regret marrying her. He already felt like his heart was held prisoner, so he should've taken his chances in prison. At least then he wouldn't have to deal with looking at her or dealing with her nagging ass mouth.

Dominick laid down on the pillow on the king size bed and closed his eyes, sending a prayer up to God before he drifted off into a deep sleep.

Father,

Please bless me with the strength to accept the things that I can not change. Help me realize that as a man it was only right to let her go and live her life the way you had written it. Thank you, father, for blessing me with the wonderful times with her. Most importantly, please let him be the right man for her."

In Jesus name, Amen.

Nessiah

Fairytales Do Exist

The sun beamed down on her tanned body as she lay face up in the sand. It was going on day ten since her and her husband had been on their one-year anniversary vacation on Cayo Largo del Sur, deep on an island in Cuba.

"Mrs. Maten, would you like a mimosa on ice?" Qaseem asked.

"Yes, Mr. Maten, I would love a mimosa," she said, smiling up at him.

She exhaled a grateful breath and then pulled her Givenchy shades from the top of her head down to shade her brown eyes. She was so happy that Qaseem had come back into her life. She thanked God every night for sending him to her for a re-do. Nessiah felt like she needed for him to embarrass her that day in high school because it made her grow a back bone. If he hadn't, there was no telling what kind of situation her naivety would've gotten her into.

She secretly prayed for God to heal Dominick's heart as well. It wasn't often that she allowed her heart to beat for him or for her mind to wander to him. She told herself the day of her wedding, a year ago, in the back seat of that limo, after she mailed off his letter, that she wouldn't allow her mind, heart and soul to hurt Qaseem ever again. She had made her decision and there was no reason to keep fantasizing about the what ifs.

Nessiah rolled over on her side and silently thanked God once again for sending her someone who valued not only her heart, but her feelings and time as well. She had just closed her eyes, when a raw and edgy, but familiar beat caught her ears. She laid there in the sand as the melody flowed sweetly into her ear drums. She didn't open her eyes, until she heard his voice. Damn, and what a sweet voice it was!

Girl, I'll still kiss your head in the morning
Make you breakfast in bed while your yawning
And I don't do everything, how you want it
But you can't say your man, don't be on it
'Cause I know true love ain't easy
Girl I know it's you'cause you complete me
And I just don't want you to leave me,
even though I give you reasons
But when it hurts,I can make it better
Girl if it works, it's gon' be forever
We been through the worst,made it through the weather
Our problems and the pain,
but love don't change.

Salty tears cascaded down her chubby cheeks as he extended the champagne flute toward her. Qaseem sat on his shins in the sand two inches away from where she laid stretched out, with three guys behind him. One with two buckets strapped around his neck, one with a set of congas and the other had an electric keyboard over his shoulder. All aiding in his creative attempt to create the beat to R&B singer Jeremih's song '*Love Don't Change.*'

"Damn, was my singing that bad?" He teased.

"Baby, that was so sweet, thank you," she said, sitting up and hugging him around the neck.

"You're welcome. I'll do whatever I have to just to see that beautiful smile," he said, kissing her passionately on the lips.

"I don't know what I did to deserve someone as special as you but thank you God for hearing my cries."

A Note From Miz. LaLa

Who knew BBW's could find love too? Everyone deserves love, not just those who are nicely proportioned. It doesn't matter if you're tall, skinny, brown skinned, the palest shade of white or some freakish green thing. Everyone deserves to have someone around that makes their whole face light up. Someone who cares about their wellbeing or just someone to be there to wipe away all the tears.

Love can be a beautiful thing if it's with the right person. Stop thinking that because you're not what society deems as beautiful, skinny or over-weight, that you must settle for mistreatment because you can't fit into a size two. Love yourself first, keep God above all else, and everything else will fall into place.

Much love!

~Miz. Lala

THE END

Coming 05/05!

CPSIA information can be obtained
at www.ICGtesting.com
Printed in the USA
LVHW111822050619
620257LV00005B/956/P